The Seven Dreamers

By Bernard St. James

THE SEVEN DREAMERS
THE WITCH
APRIL THIRTIETH

The Seven Dreamers

BERNARD ST. JAMES

PUBLISHED FOR THE CRIME CLUB BY

DOUBLEDAY & COMPANY, INC.

GARDEN CITY, NEW YORK

1982

All the characters in this book
are fictitious, and any resemblance
to actual persons, living or dead,
is purely coincidental.

Library of Congress Cataloging in Publication Data

St. James, Bernard.
The seven dreamers.

I. Title.
PS3569.A4533S4   813'.54
ISBN: 0-385-17860-3   AACR2
Library of Congress Catalog Card Number 81-43282

To my wife, Tiffany, with love

The quotation on page 117 is from the sonnet *Autunno* for Vivaldi's *Le Quattro Stagioni*. The translation is by the author.

The Seven Dreamers

CHAPTER 1

The French periodically exhibit a penchant for killing each other off. The examples that come most readily to mind are the peasant revolt of 1358 and the Saint Bartholomew's Day massacre of the Huguenots that began in Paris on August 24, 1572. Then, of course, there was the Reign of Terror, indissolubly linked with the name of Robespierre, although it was in fact a collective effort of the "Great Committee."

Following a counterrevolutionary insurrection, Lyons was destroyed by French Revolutionary troops in October of 1793, and thousands of its citizens were executed. Only two months later, a similar fate befell the Mediterranean port city of Toulon. The allies—the English, Spanish, Sardinian, Neapolitan, and French Royalist forces—had occupied the city in the name of Louis XVII since August of that year. Now the Revolutionary Army was about to recapture the port.

Shortly after midnight on December 19, 1793, there took place in Toulon Harbor and along the waterfront a magnificent fireworks display that lasted all night. Ten ships of the line were in flames, the arsenal was ablaze, and explosions rocked the ground for miles around. The English fleet was departing, and the allies had set afire those ships they could not take with them.

At dawn, as they prepared to reoccupy the city, the Revolutionary troops could see the burnt-out, smoking wrecks of the great ships standing in the harbor. They were greeted at the gate by the naval troops of Toulon, who had served the occupation forces reluctantly and tried to prevent the burning of the arsenal (so they claimed), and by part of the population. They came out to greet the revolutionaries with their band playing revolutionary hymns, carrying tricolored flags, and holding out laurel wreaths. The revolutionaries were not impressed; two hundred of the naval troops were lined up against a wall and summarily shot. And that was just the beginning.

The looting, the raping, the mass executions went on for several days. Then the formalities took over, in the form of a revolutionary tribunal and its instrument of retribution, the guillotine. After helplessly watching this bloodbath for a week and unable to put a stop to the slaughter (executions were ordered by the people's representatives of the Committee of Public Safety), the general in command of the Revolutionary troops asked to be relieved of his post. His request was denied.

One of the two people's representatives at Lyons was a former cleric turned revolutionary who was later to become minister of police in the French Empire, Joseph Fouché. Present at Toulon, and credited with formulating the strategy that recaptured the city (it earned him a promotion), was a twenty-four-year-old captain of artillery, a Corsican named Napoleone Buonaparte.

On a beautiful, sunny autumn afternoon, September 10 of the year 18—, a young man named André Corneille came to pay his respects at the house of M. Georges Pardon. The house was one of the finest on the Rue Saint-Guillaume, a fine tree-lined street of splendid houses and well-trimmed lawns. Young Corneille noticed that the curtains at the drawing-room windows were closed, which he thought rather unusual for that hour. The time was five o'clock. Nevertheless, he walked briskly up the front steps, raised the heavily ornamented brass knocker, and pounded on the front door.

There was no answer. He raised the knocker and pounded again. He could hear the sound reverberating through the entire house. But still there was no answer. That was odd indeed, for M. Pardon had assured him that both he and his wife would be at home all day. Once more he knocked, and again received no reply. Corneille shrugged his shoulders, turned around, and had already begun to descend the steps when, for no reason he could provide—then or afterward—he went back up and tried the handle. The door was unlocked.

Greatly surprised, he pushed the door inward and stepped out of the bright afternoon sunshine into the darkened foyer. He wanted to shout "Holloa!" but somehow couldn't make himself do it. Besides, his knocking before should have been enough to rouse the dead. Aside from the stifling heat—hardly surprising in weather like this, with the curtains drawn—he became aware of a humming sound that seemed to be coming from the drawing room, on the left. A low steady humming whose source he couldn't identify. Again, without knowing why, he walked on tiptoe toward the drawing room.

His eyes were becoming accustomed to the dim light. As he stood in the archway that led into the drawing room, he could make out in the semidarkness the outlines of seven people seated stiffly erect, all of them with their backs to him.

Strange, he thought. Wouldn't they have heard— then he realized that not one of the forms had moved. They were as stiff and erect as the dummy his tailor used to fit his suits. He was still standing in the archway. Now he tiptoed in and approached the nearest form, a stoutish, middle-aged man who sat there staring straight ahead at nothing, his fleshy face expressionless.

It was only when he had come around and stood directly in front of the man that the full horror of the scene hit Corneille. The man's throat was slashed, a great gaping wound that exposed the larynx. His shirt front was covered with blood, and blood had run down his cravat, over his trousers, and between his legs, forming a puddle at his feet. Flies were crawling over the open, unseeing eyes, over the torn, bloody throat, and in the puddle of blood on the floor.

Drowsy, contented flies that had been glutting themselves, probably for hours, on their rich feast. They crawled in the sticky blood, unable or unwilling to fly, and continued gorging themselves endlessly.

And Corneille knew, even without having to examine the others, that they were all of them, all seven, like this. The entire room was filled with these stiff, erect, seated corpses—and blood, and heat, and flies. Suddenly his stomach wrenched violently. He ran in panic to the front door, back out into the bright, uncaring sunlight, and stumbled blindly down the front steps. He leaned against the old elm tree, doubled over and gasping for breath, and emitted a great stream of thick, dark yellowish fluid, unaware that it was spattering over his light gray breeches, white stockings, and black leather pumps.

Finally he stopped, hoarse, exhausted, and panting. He had to get help. He had to find a policeman. It seemed to him, in his panic-stricken state, that he had been wandering about for hours, over countless city streets. In fact, it was no longer than ten minutes before he spotted a policeman and led him back to 16 Rue Saint-Guillaume.

The policeman insisted that Corneille go inside with him, but he did permit him to wait in the foyer while he went to investigate the matter in the drawing room. His reaction was much the same as the young dandy's. He too ran out, his hand cupped over his mouth, in a frantic dash for the front door. It wasn't till he was outside and had emitted his vomit that he remembered the other man. He was somewhat startled to find him standing beside him. Then he recalled his duty as a Guardian of the Peace, and asked the young man to come with him to the local prefecture. This was plainly a matter for his superiors.

Inspector Richard was out when they arrived at the prefecture of the Tenth Arrondissement. The policeman, Molles, described the scene to the sergeant in charge, while Corneille sat there wretchedly on a wooden bench, apparently in a daze. Finally Inspector Richard came in, following a dull, uneventful day, and Molles repeated his description to him. Richard looked at the young man seated on the bench, noted his white face and his stained clothes, and asked him a few simple questions. He took down his name and address and gave him permission to go home.

Inspector Honoré Richard then ordered Molles to accompany him back to the house. It was now almost half past six and the sun was beginning to set. The house itself, with its carefully tended lawn, was bathed in a golden glow, presenting a peaceful scene that belied the horrors hidden behind its drawn curtains.

Gardien Jean Molles was in a quandary. He didn't want to have to go back into that room, yet he didn't want to appear weak-kneed in front of his superior. At the same time, he was curious to see how his boss would react to this scene of carnage. He pushed open the door, permitting the inspector to enter first. He pointed in the direction of the drawing room, and again followed at the other man's heels. Molles decided to compromise by standing in the archway, entering farther only if he was ordered to do so. He tried to steel himself for the shock.

Whatever the inspector's reaction may have been, all Molles could see was the outline of an official figure moving about the room, going from one seated corpse to the next. Inspector Richard then walked quickly toward the archway, without running, holding himself perfectly erect. Nevertheless he almost collided with Molles, who was unable to step out of the way in time.

It wasn't until both men were outside on the street again that Molles saw that the inspector's face was ashen, as compared with his usual ruddy complexion. It also wasn't until then that the inspector spoke, and when he did so his voice wasn't quite steady.

"I was in the Army, but I've never seen anything like this. You stay here, Molles." Upon reflection he added, "You'd better wait inside. We don't want to attract any attention. You don't have to go into that room—my God!—you can wait at the door. If anyone should show up, detain him. I'm going to get Chief Inspector Blanc. I'm sure he'll want to know about this immediately, and he might well be home by the time I reach his house."

Inspector Richard walked several streets to the Boulevard des Invalides and tried to get a carriage. It was a bad time of day, and he had more than a little difficulty. Finally he saw a cabriolet discharging an elderly gentleman some twenty meters away, and he made a dash for it before the coachman took on another customer. He gave the driver the address, the man touched his forefinger to the rim of his hat, and then he turned front and flicked his whip at the horse.

It was a slow ride, as the vehicular traffic was heavy, and there was nothing Richard could do other than try to settle down and wait it out. The normalcy of the scene around him would never have impressed him, had it not contrasted so strongly with that terrible room. Here were men coming home from work, couples riding out for an evening of pleasure, young dandies going to see their sweethearts, or perhaps going to discover what delights and surprises the city of Paris had to offer them.

Down the Quai d'Orsay they went, across the Pont Royal and past the Tuileries. Suddenly an icy chill ran up Inspector Richard's spine as a new thought struck him. He had neglected to search the house, in violation of standard police procedure. Instead he had panicked and run outside, and right in front of that young policeman, a fresh recruit. A fine example he'd set! Of course, he'd posted Molles there, and the murderer must have gotten away hours ago. Still, it was standard procedure, and he'd neglected it. He could just imagine himself making his report, and then Inspector Blanc looking straight at him with those steely blue eyes and saying matter-of-factly, "Of course, you searched the house."

And what could he say? What excuse could he offer? Inspector Richard sighed resignedly. There was nothing to do but to go ahead and make the best of a bad job. He took out his watch as the cabriolet pulled up in front of the modest red brick house on the Rue Rameau. Two minutes past seven. The Chief ought to be home by now, if he hadn't been detained at the Prefecture. Unlike some police chiefs, he never minded missing a meal or interrupting one when he was on a case. That, at least, was something to be grateful for.

The servant opened to his knock and asked him to wait in the foyer while he went to summon the Chief Inspector. Within seconds, Blanc came out, still in his uniform, greeted Richard, and led him into his drawing room. He looked appraisingly at the taller man.

"You look as though you'd seen a ghost. You also look as though you could do with a cognac."

He went over to a decanter on the sideboard and poured a drink for his visitor. Richard took it with an inarticulate murmur of thanks and downed it with one gulp.

"Another?"

Richard shook his head. Then he proceeded to tell the Chief

Inspector his story from the beginning, commencing with young Corneille's first visit to the house. Blanc listened to the recitation without displaying a glimmer of emotion.

"We had better go there at once. I just want to give my man some instructions, and then I'll be right with you."

"I asked my driver to wait."

"You can dismiss him. Alphonse will have my horses and carriage ready within minutes, and I shall surely be wanting him later tonight as well. Émil!"

He had hardly finished calling out the name, when his servant stood attentively in the doorway.

"Tell Alphonse to get ready immediately. Then run over to Dr. d'Harnoncourt and tell him to meet me at 16 Rue Saint-Guillaume. Come, Richard, let's have a look at your chamber of horrors."

Somewhere in the house, a clock struck, and Gardien Jean Molles, already unnerved, almost jumped out of his skin. As a boy in Arles he had heard stories about people whose hair had turned white through fright or shock. He wondered if that was going to happen to him—indeed, if it hadn't happened already. As if all this weren't bad enough, it was twilight outside, and he was mortally afraid of being there alone in the dark. An older, more experienced policeman like Blanc or Richard would have noted wryly that, in his line of work, one need fear only the living. Molles, however, was not disposed to view the situation with that objectivity.

There were two candlesticks on the table, but he didn't know what the regulations were regarding such a matter. Finally he made up his mind. Surely no one expected him to stand there in pitch blackness. The sickly yellowish glow cast strange, menacing shadows around the small room. Time had lost all meaning for him, and it seemed to him as if he had been standing there forever.

Would the inspector never return? He stood facing the door in the approved position, legs apart, hands clasped behind his back. He was afraid even to turn his head toward that dark archway.

It was dark outside now. In the next room, the seven corpses rose out of their chairs. Attracted by the light, they walked slowly through the archway, their arms outstretched, ready to touch the living man, ready to take him in their bloody embrace.

Standing there petrified by fear, his body bathed in sweat, Molles scarcely heard the sound of an approaching coach and horses, or the clatter of boots coming up the front steps. Then the door burst open, and there was the inspector, along with a smaller, unimpressive-looking man whom Molles had seen before only at a distance.

Blanc looked around him at the small, dimly lighted foyer. "Light the oil lamps in every room in the house," he ordered Molles. "Including *that* one. Only, be careful not to touch anything in there."

Molles went upstairs to begin his rounds, taking one of the candlesticks with him, while Blanc and Richard waited for a few moments. Suddenly there was a rather timorous knock at the door. The two policemen looked at each other in surprise.

"That can't be d'Harnoncourt yet," Blanc commented. "Besides, when he knocks he almost breaks the door down."

He opened up, to reveal an elderly couple, who stood there blinking inquisitively at the uniformed inspector. The woman was carrying a large basket.

"I am Chief Inspector Blanc. This house is now under police jurisdiction. Who are you?"

"What— what's the matter?" the man began.

The woman gathered her faculties together more quickly.

"I am Janine Lescalles. This is my husband, Pierre. We have been in M. and Mme. Pardon's employ for nearly ten years. But what has happened? Has something happened to Monsieur and Ma—"

"Come inside," said Blanc, not unkindly. "You had better come upstairs with me."

Blanc let the old couple precede him up the stairs. Every room up here was now alight, and Molles was finishing with the downstairs rooms. The oil lamp over the staircase had also been lit. Blanc shepherded the two servants into what was presumably the study, and bade them sit down.

"What were your functions in this household?" he asked.

"I am the valet," Lescalles said. "My wife is the cook. We both share the other household tasks, cleaning, polishing, and so on."

"Are there any other servants?"

"Paul, the coachman, is hired by the month. He doesn't live here. Étienne, the gardener, is also an outside man. He comes here once a week, and he does work for all the houses on this street."

"Then, you two are the only people who live here, other than M. and Mme. Pardon. And your room is . . ."

"Downstairs, next to the kitchen."

"Have the Pardons any children?"

"No, sir." This time it was the woman who answered. "Madame never had any children. She told me so."

The two of them seemed resigned to waiting until the inspector told them what the trouble was.

"Where were you today?"

"We had been given the day off," Lescalles said. "On . . . Monday, that's right, Monday, M. Pardon told me that we could have Thursday off, after we had completed our morning chores. That meant my dusting a bit and my wife preparing food for a small party."

"Isn't that rather unusual, servants being given the day off when their employers are having guests?"

"Yes, sir, and it had never happened before. But M. Pardon knows what he wants, and I wasn't about to ask any questions."

"Didn't he give you any reason?"

"No, sir."

"Where did you spend the day?"

"With my sister and her husband in Sceaux," answered Madame Lescalles.

"You will give their names and address to Inspector Richard afterward," Blanc said.

"As a matter of fact, sir . . . ," Lescalles began.

"Yes?"

"Paul—that's the coachman—told me yesterday that M. Pardon had told him he wouldn't be needed either today."

"I have some bad news to give you," Blanc said quietly. "M.

and Mme. Pardon are both dead. They and their five guests have been murdered. Butchered would seem a better word for it."

Madame Lescalles gasped and instinctively put a hand up to her mouth. Her husband turned pale.

"M. Lescalles, I am afraid I'm going to have to ask you to identify the people in the drawing room. Presumably they were friends of your employers, and it will save us a lot of time. It's not a pretty sight, but it must be done. You, Madame, can wait up here."

Lescalles nodded mutely. He stood up, like an automaton, and followed the Chief Inspector out of the room and down the stairs. Inspector Richard and Gardien Molles were both standing in the foyer, in truth not knowing what to do with themselves. Blanc put a restraining hand on Lescalles's arm. He didn't want the old man to wander off into the drawing room by himself.

"I have already questioned M. and Mme. Lescalles," he told Richard, "but if you wish, you may ask Madame some more questions. Such as the exact date they came into this household, and the name of their previous employer. We also need the address of her sister and her husband in Sceaux, where I understand they spent the day. And, of course, whatever other questions you wish to ask."

Richard nodded and went upstairs, and Blanc led the old man through the archway. The room was now brightly lighted, and the entire scene seemed terribly unreal: the seven seated figures, the blood, the droning flies, the heat, and the sickening stench.

"The quicker the better, Monsieur," Blanc said. "Who is this?" He indicated the stout man nearest the archway.

Lescalles moved his mouth several times, but no words came out. His eyes became glazed and he started to swoon when Blanc caught him and dragged his limp body out of the room. Blanc felt annoyed at the delay, but not really surprised. He left Lescalles lying on the floor in the foyer and went to look for some brandy. Instinct told him there would be a bottle in the pantry near the kitchen, and indeed there was. He raised the servant's head and poured some of the drink down his throat. The old man coughed and sputtered, but it revived him. He blinked and looked around him in amazement.

"Shall we try again?" Blanc asked.

Lescalles nodded, and the Chief Inspector helped him up. Once more they went into the drawing room. This time Lescalles, his knees plainly shaky, managed to hold up.

"That is M. Armand," he said, indicating the man nearest the archway. "He is an old friend of M. Pardon's. That is M. and Mme. Desmans. M. and Mme. Selvay. And . . . M. and Mme. Pardon."

Blanc led the old man out of the room and back into the foyer.

"You had better rejoin your wife. I'll be up to ask you some more questions later. Also, you had better think of someplace where you two can spend the night. Obviously, you can't stay here, and I'm sure you wouldn't want to."

He ordered Molles to assist the old servant up the stairs. Then he himself went back to the drawing room. Oblivious to the heat, the stench, and the flies, he went from one corpse to another, trying to avoid stepping into the blood, but examining each one closely.

Amazing, he said to himself, positively amazing. I've never seen anything like it (unknowingly echoing Inspector Richard's first remark). All of them seated facing in the same direction, almost as if they'd been watching a performance. But whom and what? That's hardly the way people sit at a party or a little informal gathering. And why wasn't there any resistance at all? There's no sign of a struggle, and nothing in the room is upset. They just sat here, and awaited it, and accepted it.

He had the strange feeling, which he had already experienced at home when Richard described the scene, that if they could find out how it was done they would also know who had done it. He had another uncanny feeling, that time was of the essence, and that it was running out on him.

There was a clamorous pounding at the front door, and Blanc shouted out to Molles, "Open it!"

He went back to the archway. "Hello, D'Harnoncourt. I

think I can promise you something the like of which you've never seen before. I know I never have."

"Hello, Blanc. I left the most delicate, tender piece of veal on my table, because your man said it was urgent. This had better be good."

"Ah, Doctor, Doctor!" Blanc shook his head sadly. "I'm afraid old age has really caught you in his icy grip. There was a time when it wasn't a meal we had to drag you away from."

Dr. Gérard d'Harnoncourt was the police surgeon. He was also a skillful amateur artist who sketched the scene of the crime. He and Blanc had worked together on many a case, ever since the Chief Inspector had first come to Paris. There had existed, almost from the beginning, a freewheeling *bonhomie* between the two men.

The doctor marched into the drawing room and looked about him. "My God! It stinks in here!" he commented loudly. "But you're right, this is unique. The work of a madman?"

Blanc shook his head. "It looks too carefully planned and prepared for that."

D'Harnoncourt prodded and examined one of the victims, the man old Lescalles had identified as M. Selvay.

"If you get me some water," he said, "I'll wash away the blood and examine the wound. I'll try to tell you what sort of weapon he used. Rigor mortis has set in," he added.

Blanc went over to the archway. "*Gardien*," he called out, "bring us a basin of water. There's a barrel in the kitchen."

He returned to the doctor's side. "How long would you say they've been dead?"

D'Harnoncourt shrugged his shoulders. "It's hard to tell. I would think since early afternoon."

"That sounds reasonable. The two servants cleaned the place up a bit this morning, prepared some food for the guests, and were given the rest of the day off. The first witness discovered the bodies at five o'clock. But how did these bodies remain so erect before rigor mortis? You told me it takes six hours before rigor mortis begins to set in."

"Give or take a bit," the doctor amended. "As for the position, a body only needs to be propped up. If there's nothing to disturb it, there's no reason for it not to remain that way. Ah, there's a good fellow." This last was to Molles, who walked in gingerly, carrying a basin filled with water. "Don't be shy," he barked out good-naturedly. "They won't bite you."

Molles passed the basin over to the doctor and then retreated back out to the foyer. D'Harnoncourt pulled a kerchief out of his satchel, dipped it in the water, and washed the blood off the corpse's neck, meantime humming an air that Blanc recognized as being from *Richard Coeur-de-Lion*.

"I would say," he commented judiciously, "it was done with a surgeon's knife."

"Was the murderer a surgeon?" Blanc asked.

"Not necessarily. He did it with one cut, one deep incision. He might have practiced first on animals, or simply read a text on anatomy."

"That still doesn't answer our most important question," Blanc said. The two men looked at each other. "Why didn't they fight back?"

"I'll examine all the bodies when they're carted off to the mortuary. Right now I'm assuming they were all killed in the same way, at the same time, and by one person. Do you agree?"

Blanc nodded. "An attack by several people would have upset something here, and nothing is upset. Also, from the appearance of the house, nothing seems to have been stolen. No, Doctor. They were seated right as they are now when they were killed, one after the other. There was one murderer, and he used a surgeon's knife because of its sharpness and the speed with which it can be employed. Am I right?"

It was the doctor's turn to nod in agreement. "I want to examine this one some more. Then I want to examine each of them in one respect, at least. You know, of course, that just before someone is to be killed, or sometimes while he is being killed, he soils himself. After that I'll draw a sketch for you—I'm assuming you want one—and then they can take this lot away."

"I'll make arrangements for the cart now," Blanc said. He went out to the foyer and gave Molles some instructions, and the young policeman hurried off to get a horse-drawn cart from the local prefecture. Blanc decided to leave the doctor to his unpleasant task, not because he felt the least bit squeamish, but he disliked standing around with nothing to do. Again he had that strange feeling that time was running away from him. He went upstairs to join Richard and the old couple.

The three of them were seated in the study. It was obvious to Blanc that the inspector had not been wasting his time. He had drawn up a list of all the Pardons' friends. It seemed that, with the exception of M. Armand, they had other, closer friends than those who had been invited that afternoon. This, at least, according to information supplied by M. and Mme. Lescalles.

Blanc examined the sheet Richard had drawn up. "You left the house at approximately eleven, and the guests had not yet arrived by then. You had no idea who the guests were to be."

"That is correct, Monsieur," said Lescalles.

"And you returned here at twelve minutes past eight."

Lescalles looked at him inquisitively.

"I looked at my watch when you knocked on the door," Blanc explained. "Incidentally, why didn't you use the tradesmen's entrance, in the back?"

"We had forgotten the key," Lescalles said. "I thought my wife had it, and she thought I had it."

"It's probably still in the kitchen," Madame Lescalles added.

"Have you thought of a place where you can spend the night?"

"Yes, sir," answered Mme. Lescalles. "Our daughter is in service with Deputy and Mme. Fontenoy, over on Rue de la Sourdière. I'm sure they wouldn't mind if we stayed with her, considering . . . what happened here."

Blanc turned his attention to Richard. "I have no further questions for these people at present. If you're through with them, they can pack their belongings and go over to their daughter's. I sent your man back to the prefecture to get a horse cart. I want to get started on this investigation right away, and not wait till tomorrow morning. As soon as M. and Mme. Lescalles have packed and left this house, would you question all the neighbors and find out if anyone saw anything suspicious or unusual here today?"

Richard got to his feet. Blanc didn't really know the man

very well, but he was plainly conscientious and intelligent. It was also obvious, from the notes he had taken, that he knew how to question people. Like Blanc himself, he had been on duty since eight this morning. Yet he showed no signs of wanting to quit. Nor, for that matter, would any policemen with his wits about him. This was one of the most singular and extraordinary cases ever to challenge the Paris police, and a feather in the cap of the man who solved it.

As he went back down the stairs, Blanc thought about the young policeman, who had also been on duty since eight. The Chief Inspector smiled wryly to himself. That fellow was certainly getting a full dose of it, and Blanc intended to keep him going. He would learn that a Guardian of the Peace has more to do than just strut about winking at housemaids and making eyes at children's nannies.

Back in the drawing room, Dr. d'Harnoncourt was busily drawing a sketch. Blanc examined the three he had already done. They were quick but amazingly accurate drawings of the various people in the room. The one he was finishing now was a plan showing the relative positions of all seven victims in the chamber. When he finished, he looked up as if noticing Blanc for the first time. (D'Harnoncourt was a born actor, who loved to make an effect and who had missed a good career on the stage.)

"Is it all right with you if I open these curtains now?" Blanc nodded his assent. "I didn't want to touch anything before, but I think I've done about as much as I can here. A little air wouldn't hurt this place.

"Oh, by the way," he added, almost casually, "no one—not a one of them—was soiled. No urination and no defecation. They were murdered in their sleep."

CHAPTER 2

The Prefecture was buzzing the next morning with talk about the murders at number 16 Rue Saint-Guillaume. Within a matter of hours all Paris knew about the case. The *Journal* carried a full story in its afternoon edition. Their writer had succeeded in tracking down the servants, M. and Mme. Lescalles, at the residence where their daughter, Mme. Constantin, was employed as a housemaid. (That was probably Marais, their best journalist, Blanc thought. He despised the man personally, but he had to give him credit for one thing: He had a nose like a bloodhound.)

Blanc had not gotten to bed till two in the morning, but he was in his office promptly at eight. He went through a few routine reports, then got up and opened the heavy oak door. The guard outside immediately snapped to attention.

"I shall be at the Ministry of Police. All reports are to reach me there."

He walked across the street to the Ministry. The guard stationed in front of the building came to attention as he approached. There were already several people seated in the Minister's waiting room as the Chief Inspector walked right up to the large doors, knocked, and then entered.

Joseph Fouché, seated behind his large mahogany desk, looked up from the papers he had been studying.

"Ah, good morning, Blanc," he said. "I understand we have quite a problem on our hands."

"Quite a problem indeed," Blanc agreed. "Inspector Richard questioned everyone who lives on that street last night, and no one saw anything suspicious. The only people who could tell us anything are dead."

He sat down in the chair the Minister indicated.

"That wasn't the problem I was referring to. The solving of the case I'll leave to you, as always, though of course I'll be glad to give any help I can. I meant the muck the newspapers are going to stir up in their customary criticism of the police. Can't you just see their comments now: Seven citizens murdered in a respectable house, on one of the safest streets in Paris. Our citizens were previously afraid to walk in the streets; now they are afraid even to stay in their homes."

A thin-lipped smile crossed the Chief Inspector's face. "That would be Marais in the *Journal*. And of course he would be guilty of exaggeration, if not outright lying. The streets are safe. It's only when sensational crimes occur, as when that madman ran around last year throwing acid in prostitutes' faces, or like the one we're confronted with right now, that the newspapers take up the 'hue and cry.'"

Fouché shot the Chief Inspector an inquiring look.

"That's an English expression," Blanc explained.

"Of course, I'd forgotten. You're a great admirer of the English."

"Of their culture," Blanc corrected. "Shakespeare, Milton, Swift, Dr. Johnson. . . ."

"I'm only familiar with the first," the Minister said. "Nevertheless, I happen to agree with you. I believe that if our two countries, ourselves and the English, could agree on a treaty— a lasting, well-drafted treaty—we could keep the peace in Europe for the next hundred years. Well, back to the matter in hand. You know that normally I let you alone, but this is an extraordinary case. Do you have any ideas?"

Blanc reflected for a moment before answering. "I don't think it's the work of a madman. Dr. d'Harnoncourt agrees with me. The good citizens of Paris need have no fear about being murdered in their beds. The murderer of Rue Saint-Guillaume is not likely to repeat his performance, even if he could."

He showed the Minister Dr. d'Harnoncourt's sketches. He himself had written the name of each victim next to the proper figure. Blanc leaned forward in his chair. "Who were these people?"

"Georges Pardon was a diplomat. He had been the envoy to

the Court of Sardinia before he was recalled to France to be replaced by Belmont. He was awaiting another appointment by the Emperor."

The Minister, fingertips of both hands touching as if in an attitude of prayer, relayed these facts to Blanc without once having to consult his voluminous files. Blanc marveled at the amount of information this extraordinary man carried in his head.

"Lucien Armand was a contractor, that is, a civilian who supplies food for the Army. I understand he did a good job of it. The Grande Armée is unquestionably the best-fed and best-supplied force in all of Europe."

"Pierre Lescalles, M. Pardon's servant, told me that Armand and his employer were old friends."

"That may well be," the Minister said. "If their friendship goes back further than the establishment of the Empire, or at least the last period of the Consulate, my files unfortunately wouldn't tell us where and how they met.

"Albert Desmans was a lawyer. He was one of those at the Convention who voted for the execution of Louis XVI."

"Didn't you?" Blanc asked.

"Of course I did. A good revolutionary always calls for blood."

"Then, you must have known him."

"Only casually," the Minister replied. "We were members of the same party, and we were on speaking terms. That was about all. Henri Selvay made carillons. He owned the factory on the Quai Saint-Michel."

Blanc drummed with his fingers on the arm of his chair. "A diplomat, an army contractor, a lawyer, and a bell maker. What is the connection between the four?"

"Must there be a connection?" Fouché asked.

"Yes, there must. Otherwise this crime has neither rhyme nor reason. What about their three wives? Were they extraordinary women in any way?"

"You mean, was any one of them a woman with a past?"

Blanc knew they were both thinking about Prefect Dubois's wife, who had once been one of the girls of the Palais-Royal.

The Minister shook his head. "To the best of my knowledge

they were quite ordinary women, from bourgeois homes, who had been married to their husbands for many years. I don't believe any one of them had ever been noted as a great beauty or a great wit. Nor, on the other hand, did any of them have a dubious past."

"Then, we can eliminate the women and concentrate on the men. May I have their files?"

"Yes, of course."

The Minister stood up and pulled on his bell cord. The door opened and a thin young man with a long nose, who was dressed in unfashionable civilian clothing, came in.

"Devereaux, bring me the confidential files of Messrs. Pardon, Armand, Desmans, and Selvay."

"Yes, M. le Ministre."

Fouché's assistant must surely have known that those were the four men murdered in yesterday's massacre. He left the room, closing the massive door softly behind him.

"He will make a first-rate minister of police someday," Fouché commented. "He knows almost as much about this city and its inhabitants as I do. He has the knowledge and the ability. I am worried only about his ruthlessness."

Blanc looked at his superior with surprise.

"I mean, he is indiscriminately ruthless. Or he would be, given the chance. I can see that in his character right now. There are times when ruthlessness is necessary, but only when no other alternatives will work. Well, he is still young. We shall see."

There was a soft knock and the door opened again. Devereaux handed the files to his chief. The Minister indicated, with a look of his eyes, that he could go. Fouché handed the files over to Blanc without opening them. "It is something in their past, isn't it? But why the women?"

Blanc sighed and shrugged his shoulders. "We are both of us full of questions. Questions it would be better not to attempt to answer until we have more information. Good day, M. le Ministre."

The same four people were still waiting in the outer room when the Chief Inspector strode back through. Blanc's thoughts were racing as he made his way back to his own office. He understood Fouché by now, and the Minister knew him. What that worthy left unsaid was every bit as important as the things he did say. This case had first priority, and Blanc was to use every one of his inspectors if necessary. He also knew that Fouché didn't give a damn what the newspapers said: about the murders, the police, or anything else. The Minister could put a stop to that easily enough.

As he crossed the street, Blanc smiled grimly to himself. That had been Fouché's way of the letting his Chief Inspector know that his head was resting uneasily. Blanc knew he had made enemies, Prefect Dubois among them. But he wasn't the only one. There were members of the Senate, the director of the Bank of France, the Marquis de Chabrun. . . . If he didn't catch the murderer of Rue Saint-Guillaume, they could bring about enough pressure to force him to resign. And in that case there would be nothing the Minister of Police could do about it.

They stood in the Chief Inspector's office, alert, eager, and more than a little aware that they were going to participate in the case that had begun yesterday on a quiet street on the Left Bank. Blanc had called for a meeting at nine in the morning, and his three hand-picked men, Inspectors Cartier, Morel, and Dourouflé, were now standing attentively before him.

Cartier, the huge Breton, who was his personal assistant, a shrewd young peasant with the strength of an ox. Morel, a hard-bitten man of Blanc's own age, who was in charge of the notorious Ninth Arrondissement, the traditional den of Paris's thieves, cutthroats, and pickpockets. Dourouflé, a short, stout man with a double chin, whose arrondissement encompassed the Île Saint-Louis, the oldest, most aristocratic quarter of Paris.

Blanc believed that a policeman always did his job better when he knew the nature of the case he was involved with, rather than just being given a task or mission to perform. He therefore reviewed the entire story for his inspectors, beginning with M. Corneille's first visit to the house, at five o'clock. The three men gathered around his desk as he showed them Dr. d'Harnoncourt's sketches.

"And there the situation rests at present," he concluded. "Inspector Richard questioned every household on the Rue Saint-Guillaume last night. He reported back to me at the Pardons' house, which I had made my temporary headquarters. No one there had seen or heard anything. He has gone back this morning to question the day servants. The corpses were carted off to the mortuary shortly before midnight, and I expect to receive Dr. d'Harnoncourt's report this afternoon, although neither he nor I believe he will have anything significant to add.

"Inspector Richard sent one of his men around to M. Corneille's house this morning to tell him to report to me here at ten o'clock. And so, gentlemen, except for witnessing the unique horror of yesterday's scene, you know as much about this case as I do."

"How was it done, Chief?" Cartier asked.

"I don't know," Blanc replied simply.

"Could the servants have been involved?" Dourouflé asked.

Blanc shook his head. "No. I sent a man to Sceaux this morning, to check on their story. I expect him back momentarily, but I believe they were telling the truth."

"It's almost as if . . . as if. . . ." Cartier was mulling an idea over in his mind.

"As if the Pardons had done everything possible to invite their own murder," Blanc finished the thought for him. "My own theory—if indeed I could be said to have one at this early stage—is that the answer lies somewhere in the past. Somewhere in the backgrounds of these people. And so we must dig. Last night M. Lescalles gave Richard a list of all the Pardons' friends and acquaintances. They will all have to be questioned. That is what you gentlemen will be doing for the next day or two.

"Anything and everything you learn about Georges Pardon, or any of the other victims, can be of value. And of course, whether anyone has any idea what those people were doing yesterday, and why they had gotten together."

"What if it was a random, senseless slaughter?" Morel asked.

"Then, we are randomly and senselessly without a murderer. Our chances of catching him would be practically nil. Good hunting, and *bonne chance*."

The three inspectors came to attention, turned smartly, and left the room. Blanc began to study the files Fouché had given him.

Pardon, Georges Marie. Born 18 January 1756 in Lille. Son of Édouard and Marie Pardon. Father Chief Municipal Clerk. Attended Lille Academy, later University of Paris, where studied philosophy and government. Diplomatic clerk at Court of Saxony 1779, Madrid 1781. Assistant to Garron, Ambassador to Russian Imperial Court, 1784–86. Married Anne Dupont, daughter of a Rheims vintner, in 1786. Assistant to Herod in Constantinople, 1786–90. Upon return to France, allied himself with Republicans. In 1792 appointed People's Representative of Committee of Public Safety. Voted for execution of Robespierre 1794.

Upon establishment of Consulate, appointed to first full ambassadorial post, Prussia 1800–4. Ambassador Portugal 1804–7, Sardinia 1807 until May of this year.

Address 16 Rue Saint-Guillaume. No children. Friends: Tissot, Albert, Armand, Nespoulos, Borchard, Selvay, Desmans. No Royalist or Jacobin connections.

Armand, Lucien. Born 4 March 1757 in Aix-en-Provence. Son of Jean and Lisette Armand. Father a stonemason. Attended Aix common school. Originally worked at father's trade, joined Army in 1775. By time of Revolution had attained rank of Sergeant Major. Joined Revolutionary forces in 1791. Served in northern sector, later in Army of the Mediterranean, later Vendée. Rapid series of promotions, left Army with rank of Colonel in 1801.

Since return to civilian life has been contractor for food to Imperial Army. Address 44 Rue Olivier. Bachelor. Friends: Pardon, Paul Essandre, Desmans, Michel, Delbert, Roger, Carton. Has heart murmur. No Royalist or Jacobin connections.

There was a knock at the door.
"Come in," Blanc called out.

The guard entered, stood at attention, and said, "Assistant Inspector Bastard is outside, sir."

"Have him come in."

Young Bastard entered, came briskly to attention, then approached and made his report. "I questioned M. and Mme. Carneaux, Chief Inspector." (He did not dare use the more familiar "Chief.") "They're not sure of the times, but they both assert that the Lescalles spent the entire afternoon with them. They think they arrived sometime around the noon hour, perhaps closer to one. They all had dinner together. First the fish course, and then—"

Blanc put up a restraining hand. "Spare me the gastronomic details. They got there at about one and, judging from the time they returned to the house, left around six."

"Yes, Chief Inspector. That is what the man and woman said."

"I had no reason to doubt their story," Blanc said. "We just had to make sure." He drew up a list of names culled from the files Fouché had given him and gave Bastard his next assignment.

"These are friends of the Pardons' guests. Question them."

André Corneille presented himself at the Chief Inspector's office at exactly ten o'clock. He was immaculately dressed in a green dress coat, tan breeches, riding boots, a very well tied cravat with a splendid shirt front, and a brown high hat. (This last item of apparel he held in his hand.) He was far more composed than he had been the day before.

Blanc invited him to take a seat. "Are you a descendant of the great Corneille?"

"He was my great-great-great-great-granduncle. But I'm not a writer. I want to be a diplomat. That is the reason I went to see M. Pardon yesterday afternoon. I had met him and his wife a fortnight ago, at Mme. Récamier's salon. Things were a bit mobbed there, and we didn't get much of a chance to talk. I took the liberty of writing him a note, and he sent me a reply. He invited me to be at his house yesterday—September 10, that is—at five o'clock. He mentioned in his note that he was giving a small reception earlier in the day, but that it ought to be over by five."

"What sort of a reception?" Blanc interrupted him.

"He didn't specify."

"Have you, by any chance, saved that note?"

"I have it with me."

"Splendid, M. Corneille. You pay attention to details, and you may yet have the makings of a diplomat. Even if . . ." he examined the note, ". . . this tells us nothing."

"It was the most horrible thing I've ever seen, Chief Inspector."

"You're young, my friend. Give it time. Although I sincerely hope," he added as an afterthought, "that you never see anything worse."

"Am I under suspicion?"

Blanc smiled. "No. They had been dead for hours before you discovered them. And if you were the killer you would hardly have gone around the streets looking for a policeman, and then returned to the house with him. Perhaps you can help me, though."

"Gladly, Inspector."

This young man seemed to move in exalted circles. To Blanc, Mme. Récamier was only a painting. He read off to Corneille all the names, and the elegantly dressed would-be diplomat did, indeed, know a number of them. However, he had met them only socially, at the salons of Madame Récamier and Teresa Cabarrus, at Frascati's, and at the races. And, of course, he knew nothing about their backgrounds.

"Have I been of any help, Chief Inspector?"

"Your great help was in discovering the corpses. Otherwise, they would have sat there for at least three more hours before anyone found them. You are free to go, M. Corneille, and I thank you for your kind cooperation."

The two men shook hands, and the young dandy left the Chief Inspector's office. Blanc returned to his files.

Desmans, Albert. Born 13 September 1752 in Grenoble. Son of Albert and Pauline Desmans. Father a lawyer—served for period as Chief Constable of Grenoble. Attended University of Grenoble, entering at age 14. Degree in law. Practiced law locally, married Christine Jeanpère, daughter of a wealthy merchant, in 1784. Organized local Girondist party 1789, imprisoned briefly that same year, released after three months.

In 1791 elected to National Convention. Voted for conviction of Louis XVI for treason. Appointed People's Representative of Committee of Public Safety 1792. Since then has lived in Paris. Member legislature 1795–98, and again 1802–5.

Three children, Georges (born 1785) lawyer in Paris, Philippe (born 1787) lieutenant in Imperial Army, and Michelle (born 1791). Address 11 Rue Barbette. Freemason. No Royalist or Jacobin connections.

Selvay, Henri. Born 24 June 1763 in Paris. Son of Louis and Emma Selvay. Father bell maker, and both his sons, Henri and his older brother Jacques, entered family business. Both brothers joined Revolutionary Army in 1792, serving in center in defense of Paris, first under La Fayette, then under Kellermann. Jacques killed at Neerwinden 1793. Henri served in Méditerranée, later in Rhine. Demobilized 1796 with rank of sergeant, and returned to family business. Father had died that same year.

Married Claudine Manset in 1803. Three children, one of whom survived, son Louis born 1806. Factory at 3 Quai Saint-Michel. Home 3 Rue Pierre. No Royalist or Jacobin connections.

Blanc dispatched messengers to the victims' homes, and then began drawing up lists of connections between the four. In truth, Fouché's files didn't contain much, other than the bare bones. The more extensive files were kept on those people the Minister had under surveillance, those who were considered a threat to the security of the Empire.

The only thing all four had in common was that they were not in league with the Royalists or the Jacobins! Even a madman, he thought grimly, would need a better motive than that for slaughtering seven people. Pardon and Desmans had both been people's representatives, but then, so had Fouché. Armand and Selvay had both served in the Army, and both for a time in the Army of the Mediterranean—but so had thousands of others. They had also served in the defense of Paris, but in different sectors.

No, he said aloud, it's some dark terrible secret that each man had been carrying around with him. Something he never talked about. Something their wives probably didn't know about, and their children certainly don't.

Suddenly he pulled himself up short. Was he trying to read too much into this? And was he thereby missing something obvious? Perhaps the only other person who knew their terrible secret was the murderer. He read through their files again and again, made innumerable scratches on sheets of paper, and was frankly glad when midday arrived and he was able to go out to eat.

Blanc went to the small café two streets from the Prefecture that was his regular eating place whenever he spent the day in his office. Its name always amused him. It had been called the Café d'Angleterre during the all too brief Peace of Amiens. The signboard now read Café Français. It's amazing, he thought, how momentous occurrences are reflected in everyday trivialities.

The *patron*, Freire, greeted him and recommended the roast duck. Blanc had learned to value his suggestions, and found himself enjoying the dish immensely, along with rice, salad, and a bottle of Chanturgues, the Auvergnat regional wine that Freire kept in his honor. While he ate, he realized why he was enjoying his meal so much. He had never gotten to eat dinner the night before, and his breakfast had consisted of some bread and a piece of fruit.

Chief Inspector Clement came in and asked if he might join him. It was strictly a formality, done for the sake of politeness. The two men always shared a table whenever they happened to be there at the same time. Blanc liked Clement, who was in charge of the Gaming and Racing Department of the Paris Police. That was an area of sport and amusement about which Blanc knew nothing and cared even less. Nevertheless, he liked the man's bluff heartiness.

"I hear there was quite a row on the Rue Saint-Guillaume yesterday," he said.

"I wish there had been a row. Unfortunately it was all done in deathly stillness."

"Yes, you're right, of course. I understand there was no resistance at all. Is that true?"

"Seemingly, it is."

"Most unusual," Clement commented. "Highly unusual." He spoke between forkfuls of his pâté. "The most I generally have to contend with is an occasional attempt to rig a roulette wheel or doctor a set of cards. Every once in a while, though, someone works out a more elaborate scheme. The trouble is, just when you think you've learned every one of them, along comes some fellow with a brand-new idea. Still, that's not so bad either, is it? It increases one's repertoire, and one's experience. Did they have anything in common—the victims, I mean?"

Blanc had yet to make up his mind whether his colleague's blunt, open manner concealed a keen analytical mind or whether he was exactly what he seemed: a straightforward, hardworking policeman who pursued his career with great diligence and little imagination. One thing he had found was that by spreading the facts of a case out before Clement, he sometimes received a fresh idea. Or, at least, another way of looking at the same problem.

"There were four men and three women. Two of the men had been people's representatives, and the other two had been in the Army of the Mediterranean."

Clement snorted. "People's representatives! Professional spies was what they were, sent out by Robespierre to rat on an army's commander. The trouble was, they had more power than a general. Well, that's two and two. Did all four have anything in common?"

"I would imagine that all four were once in the same place at the same time. Of course, all four lived here in Paris. That is, when Pardon was not an envoy to someplace or other. But his residence was always here. I know, it is not inconceivable that they might first have met here in this city. And yet, I can't help thinking . . . when they were young and in their prime France was in turmoil, and so many dirty things were happening."

"Yes, I see what you mean," Clement said. He was attacking his veal now. "Those are things no one talks about today. It's almost as if they didn't happen—or people prefer to believe they didn't. Do you want to know what really shocked me when I was a young man? And remember, I grew up in Paris and I'd seen a lot. It wasn't so much the mob riots and murders in the streets. It wasn't the crowds that gathered to watch the mass executions—whole families with picnic baskets. No, my dear Blanc, it was seeing children building toy guillotines."

He poured himself another glass of Chambertin and studied its contents critically. "How the hell did we get onto this rotten topic?"

When he returned to his office, Blanc was torn between the desire to go out on a call and the necessity of being available in the event of an urgent message. Desire won out over necessity, and he ordered Alphonse to drive him to 11 Rue Barbette. That was perhaps too strong a word; he had no real *desire* to make this call, but he felt he oughtn't to delegate it to one of his men. Besides, there was always the possibility, however slight, that he might pick up some scrap of information to add to the pieces of the puzzle.

It was a fine house, comfortable and well kept, reflecting the lives of the people who inhabited it. A somber-looking maid answered to his knock, and when he announced himself, asked him to wait a moment while she informed M. Georges. A young man of medium height came to the door; he was intelligent-looking without being especially handsome.

"Chief Inspector Blanc," he said. "My sister received your message this morning, and she immediately sent a message to me at the lawcourts. Of course, I came home as quickly as I could. Oh, I beg your pardon. Won't you please come in."

He led Blanc into the drawing room. There a young woman of eighteen sat on a divan, a fine lace handkerchief twisted in her hands. Although her eyes were dry now, she had plainly been crying. Blanc noted the strong family resemblance between brother and sister. She, too, had an alert face, but she could hardly be described as a beauty. The two of them had probably been sitting there together for several hours.

"I must apologize for this intrusion," Blanc said. "The police are questioning everyone who knew the victims in yesterday's tragedy. I won't take up much of your time."

"Of course, Inspector," Georges Desmans said. "Won't you be seated, please. Can I get you anything?"

"No, thank you. What I'm going to ask you sounds like such a trite and obvious question, but the truth is we have nowhere else to turn. Did your father have any enemies?"

Georges Desmans laughed, a short, mirthless laugh, and then looked guiltily at his sister. "I suppose everyone who reaches a certain age has made enemies," he said.

"Of course, but is there anyone you know of who might have hated your father enough to want to kill him?"

Desmans shrugged. "He had opponents in the lawcourts. Opponents in the legislature. It's hard to believe any of them hated him—hated both our parents—enough to want to do that."

He sat down next to his sister.

"Have either of you ever met M. and Mme. Pardon?"

The girl shook her head.

"Yes, we did, Michelle," her brother corrected her. "It was quite a few years ago. You couldn't have been more than twelve at the time. We were strolling with Papa and Maman in the Luxembourg Gardens. I don't believe I've ever seen them since. He was a diplomat, wasn't he?"

"Yes. Were your parents friendly with them?"

"You'd know that better than I would," he said to his sister. "I don't spend many of my evenings here at home," he explained to the Chief Inspector.

"They've never been to this house," she said. "I don't recall my parents mentioning them in my presence."

"And yet they attended a little *fête* at the Pardons' yesterday," Blanc reminded them. "Do either of you have any idea why?"

They both shook their heads.

"Inspector," Michelle Desmans said, "can I see my parents?"

"I don't think that would be a very good idea," Blanc said quietly. "M. Desmans will have to identify them—that is a matter of law, as you well know—but I would suggest you remember them as they were when you strolled through the Luxembourg Gardens."

"We have another brother," she said. "Philippe. He's a lieutenant in the Army in Batavia. I haven't written to him yet. I'll have to do it tonight."

"Just a few more questions, and then I'll leave you alone. Have either of you ever met M. and Mme. Selvay? He was a maker of church bells."

They both looked at him in surprise.

"No, Inspector," Desmans said. "I've never heard of them. I had no idea our parents were acquainted with them."

"No, Inspector," she echoed him.

"M. Lucien Armand?"

The name evoked the same response.

Blanc stood up. "Then, I have no further questions at present."

He bowed slightly toward Michelle Desmans, and her brother stood up and accompanied him to the door.

"The mortuary is in the Hôpital des Hommes Incurables," he said to the young man. "You know where it is?"

Georges Desmans nodded.

"You can identify the bodies there tomorrow."

When Blanc returned to his office, there were still no messages for him, but the afternoon edition of the *Journal de Paris* had come out, and there was a copy of the paper lying on his desk. (He received all the newspapers every day.) The *Journal* carried a quite accurate description of the murders. Blanc, Richard, and D'Harnoncourt were prominently mentioned, but Corneille was omitted from the narrative altogether. (Naturally, Blanc thought: He had left the scene well before the Lescalles's arrival.)

The news was spreading through Paris like wildfire, he knew, and would travel across all of France. More than likely, some of the foreign papers would carry the story as well. People were the same everywhere. The public fed on sensational crimes, and the newspapers knew what to feed it.

Blanc had two visitors that afternoon, one after the other.

They were his colleagues of the night before. He had expected written messages, but the gentlemen came to report in person. First was Dr. d'Harnoncourt.

"I gave you my most sensational piece of news last night," the doctor said. "Nothing in my examinations today has given me cause to change my mind. There was some food in each of their stomachs, but of course we were expecting that. We found the remains of a meal in the dining room last night."

"Could the food have been drugged?" Blanc asked.

"You mean, in order to induce a stupor. Not very likely. They wouldn't have been sitting up, with their eyes wide open. Besides, I examined and smelled the food on the table last night. There didn't seem to be anything wrong with it."

"No, of course not. The Pardons, as hosts, supplied the meal. If the murderer had wanted to tamper with their food—I am assuming he was one of the guests—it would have been easier for him simply to poison the rest of the company and have done with it."

"By heaven, Blanc! You're right!" D'Harnoncourt looked at him as if he'd just had a revelation.

"Right about what?" Blanc asked, in all innocence.

"The murderer was not an intruder. We've already agreed on that. Therefore he had to be one of them. Someone they knew and trusted completely. The murderer was the sixth guest, and the eighth person in that room."

Blanc looked at the doctor with something suspiciously resembling a twinkle in his eye.

"You're improving, D'Harnoncourt."

"If we could only find out who that eighth person was," Blanc said aloud (he was alone in his office again), "we would have our murderer. If only one of them—Mme. Pardon, perhaps—had made a guest list. Or if either of them had told any of their friends or acquaintances whom they were inviting. . . ."

He would have Cartier make a thorough search of the house. It was worth the effort, although in truth he wasn't expecting anything. If the Pardons had given their servants the day off, including the coachman; if they hadn't told the Lescalles, who had been with them for ten years. . . .

There was a disturbance outside, in his waiting room. Blanc had half risen out of his chair when there was a knock at his door, the door burst open, and in came Inspector Richard, looking both fierce and triumphant.

"Inspector Blanc, the maid in the house across the street saw a man run out of there yesterday."

CHAPTER 3

"The stupid hussy had the day off today," Richard said. "She was the only one of all the servants I hadn't questioned, so I had to track her down. The dumb cow is sitting outside right now. Shall I bring her in?"

"Yes, by all means," Blanc said.

Richard stepped out for a moment and led in a heavyset, simple-looking servant girl who had plainly been crying. Evidently, Richard had not been easy on her.

"Sit down, Mademoiselle," Blanc said to her. "Please close the door, Inspector Richard, and take a chair yourself. Now then, what is your name?"

"Élise Ramart, sir," she said in a surprisingly small voice coming from such a large girl. She looked to be in her middle twenties.

"Where are you employed?"

"At number 11 Rue Saint-Guillaume, sir. The residence of M. and Mme. Carpon."

"You are the housemaid there?"

"Yes, sir."

"You're not married?"

"No, sir."

"Why, then, don't you live at the home of your employers?"

"I have an old, sick mother. Monsieur and Madame don't want her living in the house. I live with my mother in a room on the Rue du Maur. I go home every night and take care of her."

"Inspector Richard has told me that you saw someone running out of the house across the street, number 16 Rue Saint-Guillaume, yesterday. Is that correct?"

"Yes, sir."

"Did you mention this fact to your mistress?"

"No, sir. I. . . ."

"Yes?"

"I . . . was going to tell Madame about it. But just then Madame asked me to get something for her, and I forgot."

"Have you heard about the murders at 16 Rue Saint-Guillaume?"

"No, sir."

"Seven people were killed in that house yesterday. Therefore what you have to tell us is very important. You say you saw someone running out of the house. A man?"

"Yes, sir."

"Was he tall, short, of medium height?"

"I . . . I don't remember, sir." She hesitated for a few moments. "I think he was short."

Blanc nodded. "How was he dressed?"

"I don't. . . . He wasn't a tradesman." She screwed her face up into a grimace that looked rather comical. "He wasn't a delivery boy. He— yes, he wore a suit. But he wasn't a gentleman."

"What color were his coat and trousers?"

"I think—I'm not sure—his coat was brown. I think his trousers were blue."

"Did he have a hat?"

"Yes, sir. Now that you mention it, he did have a hat on his head. He was holding on to it as he ran."

"What sort of a hat? A tricorne, like the inspector's and mine, or a high hat?"

"It was a high hat, sir."

"In which direction did he run?"

"Toward the Rue de Grenelle."

"There, you see! You remembered a great deal more than you gave yourself credit for," Blanc encouraged her. "What time of day was this? At what time did the man run out of the house?"

"I'm not sure. . . ."

"Was it morning or afternoon?"

"Oh, it was afternoon, sir."

"What was it your mistress had asked you to get for her?"

The girl's fat, childlike face suddenly lit up. "Oh, it was Madame's medicine, sir. Mme. Carpon always takes her medicine at four o'clock. She has the gout. I saw the man running out of the house, and I was just starting to tell Madame about it when she said, 'Élise, you stupid cow'"—was that a blush spreading across her cheeks?—"'can't you ever remember to bring me my medicine without having to be told? It's after four o'clock.'"

Blanc stood up. "Thank you, Mademoiselle. You have been a great help."

"Can I go now?" she asked shyly. "I have to prepare supper for my mother."

"Yes, of course. Inspector Richard will take you back home in a carriage. If you'll just have the goodness to wait outside for a few moments. . . ." He opened the door for her.

"Good work, Richard," he said when the two of them were alone. "What made you decide to go after her?"

"I didn't want to leave any stone unturned. Her employer, Mme. Carpon, is an old crone. She neglected to tell me last night that her maid would be off the next day. When I called at her house this morning she didn't even know the girl's address. I had the devil of a time getting it."

"I'm glad you did. So far, that is the only lead we have. It may be the only one we will have."

Inspector Richard grinned. "That was good work on your part, Chief Inspector. The only thing I had gotten out of the girl was that she saw a man run out of the house yesterday and she didn't mention it to the old crone. You've gotten us a description."

"You remember the details?"

Richard nodded.

"Take her home, then go and pick up Michel. Do you know him?"

"The pickpocket?"

"That's right. He's my best informer. He knows everything that goes on in this city. He can save us several days of searching. With a little luck, and a lot of hard work, we may yet catch up with our four-o'clock man."

When Richard and the girl had gone, Blanc made several

notations in the file he had begun. He took out his watch. The time was a quarter past five. He went outside, through his waiting room and into the corridors to see which inspectors were around. Delmotte and LaFarge were both there, and he brought them into his office. There was no need for lengthy explanations, as they had both read the accounts in the newspapers.

"The maid in a house across the street saw a man run out of number 16 at approximately four o'clock." He gave them the description. "Go around to the Deux Magots, the Renard Argenté, the Café de la Victoire, and the other places. See what you can learn. And if you see Michel anywhere, bring him to me."

"Are those people likely to tell the police anything, Chief?" the swarthy Delmotte asked.

Blanc knew exactly what he meant. The habitués of places like the Victoire didn't like talking to the police.

"In this case I think we'll get cooperation. This is a sensational crime, and anyone with any tidbit to impart wants to feel important. Our main difficulty may be sifting the facts from all the rumors. There will no doubt be a reward, and you know what that always means."

Delmotte and LaFarge, who were both experienced men, did indeed know. The suspect would have been seen by dozens of people, and in a dozen places around Paris—all at the same time.

"I'll probably be here until quite late. If not, I'll leave word where I can be reached. Good luck."

Delmotte and LaFarge practically bumped into Cartier as he came in the front door, and so Blanc had another inspector to work with.

"That was a stroke of luck," Cartier said after his chief had informed him of the latest developments.

"We haven't caught him yet," Blanc reminded him. "Thanks to Richard's obstinacy and persistence, we have a lead. How did you fare?"

"Not too well, Chief. I questioned M. Tissot, Albert, Nespoulos, Borchard, Krieger, and Sordes." He referred to his notes. "They all knew Pardon a long time. Nespoulos shared a room with him when they were at the University. He only saw him occasionally these last few years, whenever Pardon was back in Paris. Tissot was the Ambassador to Saxony when Pardon was his clerk. He's a very old man now.

"None of them could think of any enemies who might have wanted to kill him. No one had any idea that Pardon was holding a reception yesterday, or who was there, or what it was about."

Blanc nodded. "I'm afraid we'll get the same results from Morel and Dourouflé. Whatever was going on at the Pardons' yesterday, they were quite secretive about it."

Cartier had been dispatched to search for Michel, and after him Morel received the same assignment. In fact, it was Delmotte and LaFarge who picked him up, at about half past eight, at the Renard Argenté, and LaFarge brought him to the Prefecture.

"You've heard about the murders in the Rue Saint-Guillaume?" Blanc asked the little pickpocket.

He had, of course, heard about them (probably before the newspapers did, Blanc thought), and that was in fact the only way Michel received his information. He could neither read nor write, but the man had an alert mind and a sharp wit.

"Four prominent gentlemen and three ladies were dispatched to that other and better world from which no traveler has ever returned." He shook his head sadly. "A terrible thing, Chief Inspector. Terrible."

"Don't start weeping," Blanc remarked dryly. "I can't stand tears in strong men."

"Of course," the pickpocket continued, "with yourself in charge of the investigation there is no question that the criminal will shortly be brought to justice."

Blanc leaned back in his chair. He felt tired. "Michel, you're going to be brought to justice one of these days. Those talented but intemperate fingers of yours will never search out another man's pockets again."

"I?" the other said in all innocence. "I am the most law-abiding man in all Paris."

Blanc couldn't help smiling. He really liked the impudent

rogue. "Of course, your two terms in prison—I'm not talking about your many arrests, or a few hours or an overnight under lock and key—were simply misunderstandings."

"Mistakes," Michel agreed, "and terrible miscarriages of justice."

Blanc was leaning back in his chair, his hands clasped together in a relaxed attitude, but the little pickpocket felt the Chief Inspector's eyes boring into him.

"You said the criminal will shortly be brought to justice. Why criminal, and not criminals? What makes you so sure there was only one?"

"According to the *Journal de Paris*—a friend of mine read me the article—there was no theft and nothing in the room was disturbed. That, at least, is what the servants are supposed to have said."

"A friend of mine also read the article," Blanc said. "Better than that, he was there last night. Now I ask you again: How do you know there was only one?"

"None of the gangs did it," Michel said quietly. "That is the word around the Ninth."

To Blanc the most important piece of information the maid had given him was that the man "wasn't a gentleman." It had been merely an observation (the girl probably wasn't allowed to express many of those), but he'd known immediately what she meant. Michel, too, wore a formal coat, trousers, and a high hat. He wasn't dressed like a worker. It was only that way that he could get close enough to a member of the gentry to relieve that worthy of some of his earthly possessions.

The Chief Inspector continued to study the other man. "Here's a bit of information you don't know. The man was seen running out of the house yesterday at four o'clock. Short, neatly dressed, brown coat, blue trousers, high hat. Still, he didn't look as if he belonged in a house like that, or in that neighborhood. What can you tell me, Michel?"

"Nothing right now, Inspector Blanc. Is there a reward?"

"There will be. One thousand francs for information leading to the capture of the murderer."

"Rest assured, sir, that should I be fortunate enough to learn of anything with regard to the despicable fellow, you will receive my information before the small hand of your splendid watch has made one half of a full circle."

Blanc was almost tempted to feel for his watch, just to make certain he still had it. Instead he laughed. "That splendid watch, which you have no doubt seen and coveted innumerable times, is a gift from the Emperor. The man who touches that, other than myself, will never see the outside of a prison cell again."

Blanc took out his splendid watch. It was nearly half past nine. He had come back from Rouen only two days before, and he hadn't seen Daphne since his return. He had hoped to see her last night. Now it seemed as though he wouldn't see her tonight either. It certainly wasn't late, but he knew that Daphne had been rehearsing all day. The Odéon began its season next Thursday, September 17, with *Sganarelle*, and the Emperor and Empress, as well as several of the ministers, were expected to be in attendance.

I wouldn't be there much before ten, he thought. But on the other hand, who knows what will happen tomorrow night, or Sunday? He was reminded of an Auvergnat saying from his youth: "It is only too late for a man after he has been laid in the earth."

He gave instructions to the guard on duty to relay all messages to his own home. Then he had Alphonse drive him to number 22 Rue Saint-Honoré. He wondered what sort of reception he would find there.

Her maid answered the door, and Daphne Perrault herself was not far behind her servant. She wore a white dressing gown, her blond hair was tied back in a chignon, and she looked lovely.

"Well," she said, looking at him with raised eyebrows, "I thought you'd forgotten me."

"There are some women, only a few, whom one never forgets. You, dear lady, are one of those few."

She led him into her drawing room and looked him over. "You look tired."

"I don't see why I should be. I got four hours' sleep last night, and none at all the night before."

"Have you had supper?"

"No, but I did eat a big lunch."

"That must have been hours ago. I'll have Clarisse bring you some cold oysters and champagne. How does that strike you?"

"Splendidly. Will you join me?"

"I'll have some champagne with you."

"What are we celebrating?"

"Your safe return from Rouen, if you like. Or, if you prefer, our reunion."

He leaned back on the divan and drank her in with his eyes. "Daphne, are you angry with me?"

"Would I serve you oysters and champagne if I were angry?"

"I remember back in the countryside we used to fatten lambs before the kill."

"You are no lamb, you're not going to get fat the way you eat, and I'm hardly likely to kill you. You can accomplish that feat yourself without any assistance whatever. You could have sent me a note upon your return."

"There, Your Grace—Your Graciousness—I plead guilty. I could and should have."

"You're impossible," she said. "And with the prominent mention you're getting in all the papers, you've become the foremost celebrity in Paris. I think all this adulation has turned your head."

At this point, Clarisse came in bearing a tray with oysters, a bottle, and two glasses. She set the tray down on a small table at Blanc's side and left the room. There was that ever-exhilarating pop, and Blanc poured chilled champagne for the two of them. They looked at each other over the rims of their glasses.

"To you and your success next Thursday, and to our reunion." He smiled. "You've been keeping this bottle for me, haven't you?"

She smiled too. "I was wondering how long it would take you to realize that."

She watched him eat. "How was Rouen?"

"Still a charming town. The cathedral still stands, as does the Palais de Justice, and their Great Clock still tells the time.

Let us not forget the spot where the Maid of Orléans was burned at the stake."

"I played there, you know. That was before we met. Not our company, just I. A guest engagement with their local theater. I was there from December to March—eight different plays in three and a half months—and when my contract had run out their manager pleaded with me to stay. I think the poor man was infatuated with me. He had a wife and four children. That is, he had given her four children, and she had three from a previous marriage. The oldest played juvenile leads, and the youngest was still being nursed."

"Was the juvenile lead also passionately in love with you?"

"Yes, as a matter of fact, he was."

"Daphne, I've always wanted to ask you this. What on earth made you choose a dull policeman?"

"Dull!" She laughed, a fine, rich laugh that Blanc always enjoyed. "You went to Rouen to break up a vicious smuggling gang that had left corpses of policemen and government officials across half of France. You've no sooner returned to Paris than you become embroiled in the most sensational murder case this city has ever seen. You see, I told you I've been following your exploits in all the papers."

"And you, what have you been doing?"

"Rehearsing. Having some new gowns made for me for the autumn by Leroy."

"Couturier to the Imperial Court, and to the courts of Cassel, Naples, Madrid, and Lucca."

She looked at him in surprise. "I didn't know you were interested in ladies' fashions."

"I'm not, really. I once investigated a crime that took place at M. Leroy's renowned establishment."

"Let me see, what else did I do to pass the time while you were away? I took lonely walks in the Jardin de l'Élysée. That's about all. You see what a dull life I lead compared with yours."

"Did you go to M. and Mme. de Luynes's reception?"

She shook her head. "I didn't want to go without you."

"You should have. You were the one they really wanted." He looked at her steadily. "I missed you, Daphne."

"I missed you."

"You were angry with me, weren't you?"

"A little."

"And now?"

It is amazing, Blanc thought afterward, how oysters and champagne can revive a man's body and spirit. Not to mention the ministrations of a beautiful and desirable woman. He was, it turned out, not nearly as tired as he'd thought.

"My God, it's disgusting. The things people do these days!"

The good woman was referring to the books she, her daughter, and her son-in-law had been examining all evening.

There had been a raid on Barba's bookshop that afternoon, an establishment which, it seems, specialized in pornographic books. The raid had been personally led by Prefect Dubois in another of his numerous morality campaigns. (This latest one had begun only this week.) He and his men had seized the damning evidence, of course, and the Prefect of Police had brought home several examples of this literary genre (the most explicit of them, in fact) to demonstrate to his wife and his mother-in-law the degenerate state of morals in present-day Paris. The three of them had spent hours perusing this shocking and scandalous material, both text and illustrations.

It was now past midnight, and Mme. Fleury announced that she was retiring to bed. Her daughter, Mme. Dubois, who had once been known as Mlle. Rosalie under the arch of the Palais-Royal (as had, in fact, her mother before her), said that she, too, was going to bed.

"Are you coming, Dubois?"

"In a little while, *ma petite*." The grossness of this intimate term of endearment, in relation to her present size, never struck her. "I still have to write my report to the Emperor regarding this afternoon's success."

She went off, and Dubois returned to the curiosity that had previously attracted his attention. Nevertheless, his mind began to wander. He had been frankly annoyed by the stories the newspapers had written about Blanc and his doings in Rouen. It seemed that one of the smugglers had a cousin there, and Blanc and Cartier had tracked the gang to the cousin's inn, where they were hiding in the cellar. One of the smugglers was killed and another wounded, and one local policeman wounded, in the capture of the gang.

Some of the idiotic journalists had presented Blanc as a hero, much to the Prefect's chagrin. He had issued a manifesto that same week—quite by coincidence, of course—that he, Prefect Dubois, would rid Paris of its crime and vice and "make of our capital truly a city worthy of our beloved Emperor."

As if all that business about Rouen weren't enough, here was Blanc's name in every paper again! Seven people murdered— all in one room at one time. Would the public be impressed now by a raid on a bookstore?

Still, if one read the accounts carefully, there seemed very little chance of success for that son-of-a-bitch this time. The corpses hadn't been discovered till hours after the murders were committed. If no one had seen anything. . . . He would have to get hold of the official police reports tomorrow.

"Damn it!" the Prefect muttered under his breath. (His wife and his mother-in-law both disapproved of swearing in the house.) That Auvergnat dog couldn't always be lucky. Why, the man couldn't even speak French before he came to Paris!

(Here Dubois was guilty of a calumny. Blanc could, indeed, speak the local Auvergne dialect, but he spoke and wrote a literate French far better than the Prefect's own, despite the latter's flowery effusions in his formal statements.)

Dubois turned his attention again to the prizes of the day's catch. There was one illustration that had especially caught his fancy. It was of a particularly voluptuous but well-proportioned young woman reclining in a most inviting pose. He looked at the drawing for some time. Then he sighed, reluctantly closed the book, put out the oil lamp, and went upstairs to join his grossly obese wife in their marriage bed.

"It's late, Michelle. Aren't you going to bed?"

"I can't sleep. I've been trying to read." She showed him the book she'd been holding, *The Sorrows of Young Werther.*

"You've read it four times."

"Six," she corrected him. "It's my favorite novel."

"Isn't it rather depressing?"

"It is." She put the book down. "I don't think anything could make me laugh tonight."

Georges Desmans, standing in the middle of the study in his dressing gown, told himself once again (as he had been doing all day) that he was now the head of this household, as he was also now in charge of his father's law office. He had a younger sister and brother to provide for. Actually Philippe was making his own way in the Army. Still, if he wanted to make a good marriage he would need more than just an officer's rank and a pretty dress uniform. Heaven knows, Paris was full of those. It was Michelle he was really concerned about. She needed to get about more, and to meet more of the right people. He would see to it, in the coming winter, that she was invited to all the proper receptions. It would also help take her mind off the tragedy.

"Georges." She looked up at him.

"Yes, Michou?"

"Why did they kill our parents?"

He sat down. "I don't know. Neither does the Chief Inspector. Papa could be a hard adversary in court—that was a side of him you never saw—but that hardly seems reason enough. Shall I tell you what I was thinking before?"

"Yes, do."

"I don't even remember what M. and Mme. Pardon looked like. That was six years ago. But I remember the feeling I got at the time, that Papa and M. Pardon didn't like each other. They had been very close once, but something had separated them. They called each other Desmans and Pardon, they introduced their respective wives, you curtsied to them—you don't remember that—but I still got that impression. That's all it was, an impression.

"Afterward, I asked Papa who M. Pardon was, but he wouldn't say anything more about him." He paused and examined his sister's face in the flickering light. "It's strange, isn't it? I mean, if our parents hadn't accepted an invitation from people they didn't much care for and whom they hadn't seen in years, if they hadn't gone to that house yesterday, they'd still be alive."

"Can I go with you to the mortuary tomorrow?" she asked.

"No." His voice was firm. "That's something I've got to do. The Chief Inspector was right. Remember Papa and Maman as they were when they were alive."

He put a gentle hand on her shoulder. "Come, Michou. Try to get some sleep."

The young woman with the reddish brown hair and the intelligent but plain face got up and did as she was bidden. Brother and sister said good night to each other as they went into their respective bedrooms.

Blanc got up at six in the morning and dressed quietly. Daphne was still fast asleep. He looked at her tenderly for a few moments and decided to leave her a note. He hastily scribbled one and put it on the pillow beside her. He went downstairs to the maid's room, where he found Alphonse in bed snoring, with one arm around Clarisse. He grabbed hold of the coachman's shoulder and woke him up.

"Hurry up and dress. We have to go back to our place."

On his way out, he picked up his tricorne and sword, which Clarisse had taken from him upon his arrival the night before. Dawn had already broken over the city of Paris. As his coach rattled along the Rue Neuve de Luxembourg, Blanc watched the grocers and fruit sellers making ready to open their shops, sweeping and preparing their wares for display. In the houses, lattices were being opened to greet the morning. The streets were already alive with people on their way to work. He liked watching the city wake up. Whatever his mood, whatever the circumstances of the night before, it was a sight that never failed to inspire him. No, he had never regretted coming to Paris, not for one moment.

They arrived at number 8 Rue Rameau. There were no messages. Blanc shaved, took a bath, put on a fresh uniform, and went downstairs to a breakfast of oranges, fresh croissants, and hot coffee. Émil officiated inconspicuously in his household. He had drawn a bath as soon as he saw the coach clattering down the street, and then had gone out for some croissants. Alphonse might or might not say something to his manservant, but even if he didn't, Blanc had not the slightest doubt that Émil knew where he'd spent the night. Émil knew everything. *He* ought to be Chief of Police, Blanc mused.

He arrived at his office at precisely eight o'clock and went through the routine reports he found on his desk. There were also reports from Morel and Dourouflé, who had had no better luck than Cartier. There was nothing to wait around for. He might as well let Morel and Dourouflé go back to their own prefectures. He himself would visit as many of the local prefectures in the twelve arrondissements as he could manage, to see how they had been holding up since his return to Paris. These unexpected and unscheduled tours of inspection were his way of keeping his men alert.

And so Saturday, September 12, passed in a routine manner.

At 4:15 A.M. on Sunday, Blanc had an unexpected visitor at his house. It was Michel, in a high state of excitement. Blanc put on his dressing gown and went downstairs to his drawing room, where the little pickpocket was sitting uncomfortably under Émil's watchful eye, fidgeting in his chair.

"I kept my word to you, Inspector Blanc, that as soon as I received any information I would immediately report to you."

His hands were playing nervously with his hat, which he kept on his lap.

"Tonight, or rather, this morning, at the Café de la Victoire, Léon the Frog was babbling somewhat incoherently about blood and corpses. It seems he was somewhat in his cups. I wasn't present myself, but I have it on excellent authority that this was so. According to my unimpeachable source of information, he had never seen Léon so frightened before. He acted as if he expected a ghost to walk in through the door."

Blanc nodded. "Where does Léon live?"

"Nineteen Rue des Écouffes, Chief Inspector. On the third story, the first room to the left of the staircase. There's no room number."

"Very well. Go on home now."

Michel was ushered out into the dark blue night. Blanc felt that his orders to Émil were superfluous. He merely gave them for the sake of form.

"Emil, wake Alphonse and tell him to get ready."

He himself went upstairs to dress. Within a few minutes

Blanc was seated inside his fine coach, an erect figure in his blue dress uniform with its ornate gold braid, tricorne set firmly on his head, holding on to the handle of his sword, while Alphonse sat up on his box, urging the pair of horses on, as the coach careened off into the dark blue of the Paris night.

CHAPTER 4

Rue des Écouffes, which leads to the Rue du Roi de Sicile, was not the sort of district in which any sensible person would wander alone at night. Blanc saw no point in having Alphonse wait for him. Besides, the sight of a coach standing outside the house might well frighten Léon off, in the event that he should come home.

"Come back for me at nine," he ordered the coachman.

He stood for a moment watching the coach clatter off into the night and then went through the archway into the courtyard to rouse the concierge. He pounded and pounded on the door of the lodge, knowing that someone was inside, sleeping heavily and probably drunk. After what seemed like an eternity he heard someone moving behind the door.

"Who's there?" a woman's voice asked. It sounded hoarse.

"Police. Open up."

The door opened a crack, and Blanc caught a glimpse of a woman standing in her nightdress, holding a candle. The chain was still on the door.

"What do you want?"

"I told you. I'm a police inspector. Open the door."

She moved the candle up and down so that she could examine him, and saw that he was indeed in uniform. The door closed, there was the sound of a chain being unlatched, and then the door opened again.

"Why are you bothering law-abiding people in the middle of the night?" There was a sour smell of wine on her breath.

"A man named Léon lives here. Léon the Frog. Is he home?"

"Maybe, and then again, maybe not."

"I asked you a question."

"M. Léon isn't home yet. He didn't come home last night, either. What's he done?"

Blanc ignored her question. "Let me into his room."

"Just a moment. I'll light the oil lamp and get my key."

Blanc stepped inside as she moved away from the door, and looked around him at the small room. Against the wall stood the bed from which she had just gotten up, and in the middle of the room was a table with the remains of a meal and an empty wine bottle. She came back, still holding the candle and with a shawl draped over her nightdress. She seemed about fifty, with a lined, yellow face and long, straggly hair streaked with gray. Possibly she was younger than she looked.

"Are you married?"

"Why do you ask?"

"I thought your husband might know Léon."

"My husband was killed at Hohenlinden. I lived with another man for a while. A carter. He left me." Her hoarse voice was empty of any emotion. "Shall I take you upstairs?"

"I know where his room is. Just give me your candle and the key. Understand one thing, Mme. . . ."

"Plessart."

"Mme. Plessart. If Léon should come back, and if you breathe one word to him of my presence in his room, it will mean a long prison sentence for you."

"It's serious, then."

"Very serious. My advice to you is not to get involved."

"I'm going back to sleep. If M. Léon comes home, I'll let him in, but I won't tell him you're upstairs."

"That's right."

She unlocked the door of the house for Blanc and closed it again after him. On the other side of the door he could hear the door of her own lodge closing, and the sound of the chain being latched once more. He held the candle in front of him and proceeded to climb the pitch-black stairs. Each step of the old stairway creaked under his feet. Judging from the style of the house, with its enclosed courtyard, it had been built in the sixteenth century and had once contained apartments for courtiers, soldiers, and government officials. Now its rooms had been partitioned and made smaller, and that was probably all the work that had ever been done there since the original construction.

He came to the landing on the second story, where it was still pitch black, and then continued on his way up the stairs. So Léon had not come home the night before, either. The man must really be frightened. For two days he had wandered around, keeping his terrible secret to himself, until at last, in the early hours of Sunday morning at the Café de la Victoire, drunk and half crazed with fear, he had blurted the whole thing out.

Blanc reached the third story. Michel had said the first room to the left of the staircase, but he turned around first, holding the candle every which way, to make sure there were no spying eyes. No, all the doors were shut, and from behind one of them he could hear deep, contented snoring. He tried the key in the lock and it fit and turned easily. He let himself into the room and shut the door behind him.

Léon's room was sparsely and simply furnished but surprisingly neat and clean. Like Michel, he was obviously a man of fastidious habits. Blanc put the candle on the table and sat down in a chair. The bed was properly made up, and the room contained a wardrobe, a dresser, and an old but polished mirror. The curtain at the window was drawn, so the light of his candle couldn't be seen from the courtyard below.

Blanc went over to the window, parted the curtain slightly, and peered out. The first dawn was in the sky, and the courtyard was still deserted. The concierge was probably snoring again in her bed. Looking out at the scene, he could imagine Cyrano galloping out on horseback through the archway, and on down the cobblestoned street, possibly on his way to fight one of his constant duels. A romantic vision, no doubt, but it must have been that way once. Now this was a ruin of a house sheltering the ruins of people.

For lack of anything better to do, he turned the room upside down. He searched quietly and efficiently, under the goose-down mattress, behind the bed and underneath it, in every drawer of the dresser, between the drawers, behind the dresser, inside and on top of and behind and under the wardrobe. He took the mattress apart. There was nothing. Like

Michel, Léon was too smart to leave any stolen items in his room for the police to find. He probably sold them to old Pétain as soon as he acquired them.

Blanc couldn't help smiling grimly at the thought of the withered yet ageless fence who practically ran the Ninth Arrondissement and with whom Morel had been engaged in battle for years. So far neither side had won. And though it was unlikely that Pétain would win this war, the police had never been able to convict the old scoundrel of any of Paris's numerous thefts, or for the great quantities of stolen goods that regularly passed through his hands. Whenever Morel and his men raided one of Pétain's reported hiding places, they found nothing but an empty warehouse.

And yet, Blanc told himself, we will get him. Patience and persistence would win out in the end. That is, if Pétain didn't die of old age first.

Blanc continued to pass the time in this way, entertaining himself with his own thoughts. His candle had burned down and it was light outside now. The daylight filtered in even through the drawn curtain. He looked at his watch. Half past six. He got up and went over to the window again. The courtyard was still deserted. His vision of the past had been wrong in only one respect, he mused. Cyrano would not have fought a duel on Sunday morning.

He returned to his chair and sat down again. Léon the Frog had gotten his name when he once jumped from a second-story window, over the heads of the policemen who were coming to arrest him, and scampered off to safety. But that had been quite a number of years before. He couldn't be that active any more, and this room was on the third story. Nevertheless, Blanc was determined that, if the man should show up, he would not slip away from him.

He went over to the window and peered out again, cautiously, without moving the curtain. However exhausted Léon might be, he was an old professional, and the first thing he would do upon arriving home would be to look up at the window of his room for any sign of movement. But no, there was still no one about. The entire house was asleep, and so, it seemed, was the neighborhood.

Blanc was content to sit down at the table again and bide his time. He had replaced the blanket over the bed, as neatly as he could, lest Léon, opening the door and seeing the disarray, bolt down the stairs and run back out into the street. Why put the entire Paris police to work hunting down one man when a single inspector could do the job? Always provided, of course, that Léon did come back.

Blanc took out his watch again. It was half past seven. Suddenly he sat up straight, stiff and alert. There was a creaking on the stairs. It was a soft tread, but there was no way anyone, even an acrobat, could make his way up those stairs quietly. He stood up, tiptoed over to the door, and remembered just in time to take his tricorne off the table and toss it behind the bed. He flattened himself against the wall beside the door as a key was stuck into the lock, there was a click, the handle turned, and the door opened slightly.

A man's arm came into view. Blanc grabbed hold of the wrist, twisted, and pulled the man into the room. Léon the Frog, a small, slender man, was wearing a brown coat, blue trousers, and a high hat. His cravat and shirt front looked as though he hadn't been home in two days. The man was exhausted and offered no resistance. He seemed, in a way, relieved that it was over.

Blanc closed and locked the door. "Sit down on the bed, Léon. Lie down, if you want to. Is it necessary for me to tie your hands and feet, or do you give me your word you won't try to run away? In that case, we shall have to track you down, and we will find you."

Léon sat down on the bed, took off his hat, and buried his face in his hands. "I won't run away," he murmured.

"Why didn't you leave Paris?"

Léon looked up at the Chief Inspector, who had seated himself in the chair. His face bore an expression of incredulousness. "I was born here. I don't know any other place."

Blanc was not surprised at the man's answer. Most criminals felt that way; they spent their entire lives in one city. "Yes, that's true. Paris is your home, as much as it is mine. Perhaps even more so."

"I came back here because I had no place else to go. I suppose I knew you'd catch me—sooner or later."

He sounded as if he were talking in his sleep. Suddenly his voice took on an urgency, a sincerity that could only have been born of despair. "Inspector Blanc, my mother is buried in the Cimetière du Sud. I swear to you, upon her grave, I didn't kill those people."

The Chief Inspector's quiet reply must have astonished him. "I know you didn't."

"Then, why—"

"You, my lad, are an official suspect. The only official suspect we have at the moment, and the papers, with their motley, ink-stained scribblers, must be appeased."

"Will I . . . ?" He made a cutting motion with the edge of his palm against his neck.

"You may sit in prison for a while, but I don't think you and your head will be parting company."

Léon the Frog looked relieved. For the first time in three days, the strain and anguish left his face.

"Shall I tell you what happened?" Blanc said. "On Thursday, September 10, you were wandering around the Tenth Arrondissement, scouting the territory for a house to rob. Walking down Rue Saint-Guillaume at about four in the afternoon, you passed a residence that had its curtains drawn, at least in one room. Your curiosity got the better of you, and you couldn't resist trying the front door. Need I go on?"

Léon shook his head. "You're right, Inspector Blanc. That's exactly what happened. When I saw those . . . dead people sitting there . . . I just ran. I couldn't go to the police—you understand that—and I prayed no one had seen me. Now I suppose we'll be going to the Prefecture."

"In a while. My coach is coming back for me at nine o'clock. In the meantime, if you want to sleep, I have no objection."

"Thank you, Inspector Blanc." There was genuine gratitude in Léon's voice. "I would like to take a rest."

"Look at it this way, Cartier," Blanc said. "Léon the Frog is a professional thief. He is a burglar by trade, as Michel is a pickpocket."

It was Monday morning, and the two men were seated in the Chief Inspector's office.

"Léon makes a specialty of robbing the homes of people who are away from the city—or, in some cases, people who are merely out for the evening. Like Michel, he doesn't carry a weapon. Neither man has ever killed anyone in his life.

"And now that we've looked at the man, let us examine the crime. Seven people killed in one room, in a mass murder which, we are all agreed, was carefully planned and meticulously executed. Would the man who cold-bloodedly plotted and carried out this scheme then have panicked and run out of the house like the proverbial chicken around the farmyard? I think that sort of person would be far more likely to walk out the front door casually and simply stroll away in the manner least likely to attract attention."

"Do you think Maître Alain could make out a case against Léon?" Cartier asked.

Raymond Alain was the sharpest, most able prosecutor in Paris. He and Blanc had a long relationship, working sometimes with and sometimes against each other.

Blanc couldn't help chuckling at the thought. "Léon's record would unquestionably count against him. And that despite the fact that he would be the last person to murder seven people in a house and steal nothing. Incidentally, how did he get them to sit still for him? But, in any case, Maître Alain will not get the chance to practice his formidable skills against Léon."

"We have no other suspect," Cartier said.

"Indeed we don't," Blanc agreed, "and it is for that very reason we cannot permit Léon to be tried. His trial and conviction would close this case. That would merely becloud the issue and prevent us from tracking down the real killer."

"Then, why hold Léon, Chief?"

Blanc shrugged his shoulders. "For one thing, he is guilty of illegal entry. For another, he is, as you said, our only suspect. No, Cartier," he concluded, "Léon will not stand trial, but I think we shall keep him for bigger and better things."

"You're certain the man didn't do it?"

"Absolutely, M. le Ministre."

"Do you think Maître Alain could get a conviction?"

Interestingly, Fouché asked Blanc the same question Cartier had previously posed.

"He probably could," Blanc replied. "Léon would be hard pressed to prove his innocence, even with the best lawyer in all of Paris defending him. Ironically enough, that would have been Albert Desmans only a few days ago."

"I understand you want to hold the man anyway."

Blanc nodded. "We must. I need an official suspect. The newspapers must be informed that we have Léon and that he was seen and identified as the man who ran out of the house that day. That will appease the critics for a while. Even more important, it may help in our search for the true Murderer of Rue Saint-Guillaume."

"You mean," Fouché said, "it may well bring him out of hiding if he believes the police have latched onto some poor dupe."

"I'm not sure he is in hiding," Blanc commented wryly. "He might be strolling about the streets right now. But it may make him careless."

The Minister of Police played with one of his quill pens. "As far as I'm concerned, you can hold him. I'll feed the proper stories to the newspapers. But let me ask you one question, Blanc. Suppose you don't find the real murderer, what then?"

Blanc met the Minister's eyes evenly with his own. "I won't press charges against Léon."

"You mean, you'd sooner admit the police had made a mistake, release Léon, and end your career?"

"I can't let an innocent man be tried and convicted."

"Damn it, Blanc! The man's not innocent."

"Not of other things, perhaps, but he is innocent of murder, and that's what concerns us right now."

The Minister shook his head incredulously. "Somehow, I knew that would be your answer. You know, Blanc, I'm surprised you've lasted this long."

"So are a lot of other people. But we are the Guardians of the Peace. I wish we had been given the title Guardians of Justice. And law without justice, without truth, is worth nothing."

The Minister chuckled. "In some ways you remind me of my

late colleague, and friend, and sometime enemy, Thomas Paine. I presume you've read his work."

"*The Rights of Man.* Yes, I have. I didn't know he'd died."

"Last year, in the United States. I understand he was almost forgotten there. There ought to be a lesson in that for all of us."

"But *The Rights of Man* isn't forgotten."

"No, it's not," Fouché agreed. "And it probably never will be. All right, Blanc, if you want to make a martyr of yourself I can't stop you. I only hope, for your sake, you catch him: the Murderer of Rue Saint-Guillaume."

The afternoon papers carried the story of Léon's capture, nor did they neglect to mention the fact that Chief Inspector Blanc of the Criminal Investigation Department had managed the capture single-handedly. Blanc couldn't help snorting derisively. It took more courage to cross the Champs Élysées at five in the afternoon! Nevertheless, he had to admit that Fouché had done his part admirably. Léon's name had to be kept alive in the papers, with more spicy details added daily. Fouché was, he knew, good at that sort of thing. Invention especially seemed to be his strong point. The man could have made a successful career as a popular novelist.

Once again Chief Inspector Blanc was the hero of the day. He had solved this unique and sensational crime in three days, and once again Prefect Dubois fumed. Seated in his large, ornate office, he directed every epithet in his vocabulary against that Auvergnat dog. The man had the damnedest luck! And yet, once his choler settled down, the Prefect began to experience some gnawing doubts. He was neither an intelligent nor a cultured man, but he had an instinctive shrewdness that made him a dangerous enemy.

The whole thing seemed too quick, too easy. A man conveniently seen running out of the house, immediately and easily identified (Fouché had kept Michel's name out of the story, in order to retain his value as a police informer) and then taken prisoner in his own room. Finished, boxed, and tied with a ribbon, like the hats his wife liked to order from Mme. Fabien.

No, he decided. Even that son-of-a-bitch couldn't be that lucky.

He had to know more. For some reason that he himself couldn't have explained, Prefect Dubois had become obsessed with the case. The official police report hadn't told him enough. He needed, once more, to have a look at Blanc's confidential files. So far he hadn't found anything in his life, professional or private, to warrant his going to the Minister, or to the Emperor himself. He wasn't in league with any of the Empire's enemies: That much had been established. And if he were, Fouché would be the first one to know about it. So far, he had managed to avoid all scandal. But . . . damn it! There had to be something!

Dubois rang for his assistant, Inspector Desny. When that individual entered his office, the Prefect wrote a name down on a slip of paper and showed it to the other man.

"Tell him I want him in my office after he goes off duty."

When his inspector left, Dubois returned to the proclamation he had been working on, which he intended to send to the newspapers after he had polished and reworked it to his satisfaction.

"Severity but humanity! My eye shall penetrate the innermost recesses of the criminal's soul, but my ear shall be open to the cries of innocence and even to the groans of repentance. . . ."

Dubois had to admit to himself that he liked it. The words had a rolling grandeur to them. He continued working in this manner until, shortly after six, there was a discreet knock at his door.

"Come in," he called out. He continued writing and then looked up, as if noticing his visitor for the first time. The man saluted smartly and then stood erect, feet apart, hands clasped behind his back, awaiting the Prefect's orders.

"You're certain no one saw you enter this office?"

"No one, M. le Préfet."

Dubois nodded and grunted. "I need his confidential files once more," he said. There was no need for the other to ask whose files he meant. Nevertheless, he started to look extremely uncomfortable. Dubois, who was a shrewd observer of his fellowman, knew the man was frightened. He also knew, as the other did, that he was in too deeply to refuse him this time.

"I especially want those files about the seven people who were murdered, and the prisoner they have. Is he working on any other case right now?"

"No, M. le Préfet."

"Then, get those files and bring them to my home tonight. The same procedure as last time."

It was certainly not a hot day, nor was it hot there in the Prefect's office. Nevertheless, the man was sweating profusely. Had he not still kept both hands clasped behind his back, he would no doubt be tugging at his collar. Dubois regarded his man evenly. He knew how to inspire fear, and also how to fan the fires of greed.

"Of course," he said almost casually, "there will be payment made for services rendered. The same amount as last time."

The man nodded mutely. Then he found his voice again. "One more time, then."

"Of course," Dubois assured him. "One more time. Look, my friend." He leaned forward, as if taking the other into his confidence. "You can only profit from your service to me. I'm not the man to forget. When our Chief Inspector in charge of the Criminal Investigation Department becomes the former Chief Inspector, you'll get a promotion, one that's been long overdue. You have Prefect Dubois's word on that."

"Thank you, M. le Préfet."

Dubois waved his hand magnanimously, as he had seen Talma do it on stage when he had played some king or other. He turned his attention back to his proclamation, thereby indicating that the interview was at an end.

The man who had become the police's Official Suspect, Léon Frennel (he himself had almost forgotten his last name by now), better known as Léon the Frog, was becoming ever more prominent in France. The provincial newspapers took up the story from the Paris papers and made much of the case. Frenchmen everywhere could get all the fascinating details over breakfast or, if they preferred one of the afternoon papers, over their glass of wine or brandy at their favorite café.

Needless to say, the case provided lively subject matter for after-dinner discussions, when the experts had *their* say.

Fouché continued to feed a steady stream of lurid material to the Paris editors, much of it of his own invention. Privately he shook his head. Blanc was getting himself in deeper and deeper. But he had promised the man cooperation, and cooperation he would give. He was fully aware, he wryly told himself, that if his Chief Inspector didn't bring this off, he himself would not come out of the affair looking terribly good.

Had Dubois been in charge of this investigation, he knew, he would have fastened onto the first likely suspect—that is to say, Léon the Frog—gotten a conviction, and basked in the glory of a difficult case quickly and sensationally solved. But Blanc was never one to do things the easy way. He really did resemble Thomas Paine in his determination to be unpopular with those in authority.

"Ah, well," the Minister said aloud with a sigh, "I chose the man, and I suppose the least I can do is support him if he feels that strongly about it. I only hope I have no reason for regrets afterward."

Inspector Blanc, too, felt far from jubilant as he perused the daily papers. Their praises had, for him, a hollow ring, and a mocking one. A week had gone by since the discovery of the corpses, and all his and Cartier's investigations had turned up nothing. A thorough search of the Pardons' house had disclosed no guest list—no hint of how or why these particular people had been chosen. All the questioning of the victims' friends and relations had proved fruitless.

"Something is missing from the puzzle," he told himself. "Or perhaps I've merely overlooked something. When Richard burst into my office that day with his astounding news, I thought it was so miraculous, events working in our favor for a change, I suppose I must have stopped thinking. It's time to start again," he concluded, "and go back to the beginning."

He returned to his files, Dr. d'Harnoncourt's sketches, and his own indelible impression of that room, and went back to the beginning.

As for Léon the Frog, he was resting, in fairly reasonable comfort, in a cell in the old Prison de l'Hôpital de la Pitié. He had been brought several changes of clothes from home and was able to take full baths in a water barrel placed in his cell. Thanks further to Blanc's intervention, the food he received, though not delectable, was certainly not slops. The bread, moreover, was very good.

He read the papers carefully, as he did every day, over his breakfast. A breakfast of warm crescent rolls with freshly churned butter, fruit preserves, aromatic hot coffee that had been ground only moments before it was brewed, and warm thick cream that had been brought into the city that very morning from one of the surrounding farms.

Breakfast finished, he got up and commenced his toilette, assisted by his valet. He put on a shirt of splendid silk—Lyons silk, he mused—with a ruffled front and finely starched cuffs. Then a handwoven cravat, unostentatious but expensive to the discerning eye. His man handed him his stickpin, which encased a magnificent diamond that had once been owned by Cagliostro. He adjusted his hair, worn shoulder length in the fashionable manner. Then his coat, his walking stick with its carved ivory handle, and his high hat (which his manservant again brushed off with his sleeve before handing it to his master).

His concierge greeted him ecstatically as he passed her open door, and he tipped his hat to her in a manner that made her heart flutter. This was his unchanging daily routine whenever he resided at home, but it inevitably provided the highlight of the young woman's day. On the wide, sun-drenched boulevard, people smiled and nodded at him. Those who knew him greeted him by name. Those less fortunate, who knew him only by reputation, also smiled and inclined their heads.

The ladies—those out strolling with their maids in tow, and the young girls chaperoned by nondescript elderly spinsters—turned their heads and looked at him admiringly. Though not a tall man, he was well built, carried himself erectly, and wore clothes with style and elegance. His most outstanding feature was his eyes. They seemed to burn and penetrate into the person he looked at, and women of all ages and classes considered him a romantic man.

Even though it could hardly be considered morning any more, he took what he called his regular "morning constitutional," strolling around his favorite streets. He made several stops, calling on friends and business acquaintances, with one of whom he had lunch. By midafternoon he had arrived at his favorite cafe, where the proprietor and all the waiters knew him. His regular waiter knew exactly what to bring him: Turkish coffee and a magnificently lavish dessert, followed (after a discreet length of time) by a cognac. This was, in effect, his headquarters, where he spent almost every afternoon, meeting friends, conducting his business affairs, and reading all the afternoon papers.

He was the Murderer of Rue Saint-Guillaume, and he walked about the streets without fear and with absolute confidence, secure in his knowledge that he would never be brought to justice.

CHAPTER 5

At eight in the morning on Tuesday, September 22, Inspectors Coimbeau and Cartier presented themselves in Blanc's office, both sporting wide grins.

"You've got to see this, Chief," Cartier said, barely able to contain his mirth. "It beats anything I've ever seen."

"It starts at Passy," Coimbeau began—but Cartier silenced him with a poke in the stomach.

"Don't. You'll ruin it for the Chief."

Blanc, seated behind his large mahogany desk, looked up at his two inspectors. He hesitated for a fraction of a second, and then reached out for his tricorne, which was sitting on the edge of his desk. "Very well," he said. "I suppose I could use a good laugh." He stood up and buckled on his sword, whose scabbard had been slung over the back of his chair.

The three of them traveled in Blanc's coach, the two inspectors, who sat facing their Chief, smirking like schoolboys all the way. Blanc was already beginning to have an inkling of what this was all about, but he kept his suspicions to himself in order not to spoil his men's enjoyment. They reached Passy, at the barrier, in something under half an hour, and climbed out in front of a two-story wooden house.

"This," Cartier said, sounding like some sort of guide, "is the residence of Citizen Lanchère, who claims he knows nothing about it. He says he's innocent as a newborn babe." He joined his fingers together as in an attitude of prayer and cast his eyes heavenward. Both he and Coimbeau burst into raucous laughter.

"Let's go into the cellar," Coimbeau said.

The two policemen standing guard in front of the house snapped to attention as the three inspectors approached. They

went inside, and Coimbeau and Cartier led Blanc to the door
that opened onto the cellar. Coimbeau, who considered himself the leader of this expedition, as the whole thing was his
discovery, lit an oil lamp and led the way down a rickety flight
of stairs, with Blanc following and Cartier bringing up the
rear. Several oil lamps were flickering down there, casting the
men's shadows about in a most impressive way. All the walls
were completely lined with kegs, and the place reeked of
brandy, in a manner to delight the most ardent *ivrogne*. The
smell had hit Blanc at the top of the stairs.

"Charentes cognac," he said. The other two nodded.

"There have been seventeen of these reported this year
alone," Cartier said, "but this one is really a masterpiece."

"They must have worked at it for months," Coimbeau added.

At the end of the long room, resembling a large mousehole,
was the black entrance to the tunnel. Blanc and Cartier each
picked up an oil lamp and, with Coimbeau again leading the
way, they crouched low and entered the passageway. They
looked and felt more like miners going to the coal face than
police officers. Miners are traditionally short men, and Cartier
was 193 centimeters tall when standing erect. He was bent
over almost double in this cramped space and was by far the
most uncomfortable of the three.

"I am reminded of the Turks when they tried to tunnel their
way into Vienna underneath the city walls some two hundred
years ago," Blanc remarked.

"The best is yet to come," Cartier said between grunts.

"Wait till you see where we end up," said Coimbeau.

They were following a conduit that seemed to stretch, outside their small circle of light, from black infinity to black
infinity. Blanc knew they had passed underneath the barrier
and were well inside the city by now, but he had lost all sense
of direction. It was nothing short of a miracle that the "moles"
had maintained theirs.

"How long is it?" Blanc asked.

"Two hundred seventy-three meters." The answer came
from Coimbeau's back, which was directly in front of Blanc.
"I've named it 'The Gallery.'"

"A good name," Blanc commented. "Our smuggler friends

also borrowed a leaf from the ancient Romans, some of whose conduits are still in use in southern France today. Except that those, I believe, were constructed to convey water."

The "moles" were certainly a nuisance, and a costly one to the Excise, although their ingenuity supplied the police with considerable amusement. The real source of concern were the brigands, the smugglers who plied their trade aboveground. Their ranks included unemployed workmen, vagabonds driven out of the countryside, military deserters, and cashiered army officers. They had taken the Porte de Fontarabie by assault, fatally shot a policeman at the Barrière de Neuilly, and killed two more policemen on the Pont de la Liberté. The customs employees were not part of the police, and so the brigands only came under Blanc's jurisdiction after they had committed a capital crime.

Finally the tunnel led them into another cellar, where they were able to straighten up and ease their aching backs. This place, too, reeked of cognac, had kegs piled all around, and had several oil lamps burning. These last had been supplied by the police, who had also emptied the contents of all the kegs into huge barrels, which had been carted off to Coimbeau's local prefecture (this on the advice of Cartier, lest brandy kegs suddenly begin mysteriously "disappearing"). And so this latest pipe system of the "moles" had ended its active days, and the precious liqueur was gone, but the aroma lingered on as a fragrant memory.

Cartier was aching to divulge their present location to his Chief, but this was Coimbeau's case.

"Well, Chief Inspector," the latter asked, "where do you think we are?" Blanc shrugged his shoulders and waited for the joke to explode. "We are now standing in the cellar of the Convent of the Filles-Sainte-Marie."

"At Chaillot," Cartier added.

There was loud laughter, and Blanc couldn't help smiling.

"Did the good sisters know about this?"

Coimbeau shook his head. "I don't think so, Chief. It was one of them who reported it to me. Sister Marie Joseph claimed she'd been hearing voices. She was admonished by the Mother Superior for trying to emulate Jeanne d'Arc, but she persisted, and finally the matter was brought to my attention. Here, I'll show you how they brought the kegs out."

He led the way to a door, practically hidden in the darkness, lifted the heavy bolt, pulled up the handle, and drew the door open. The policeman stationed outside jumped with surprise, which he quickly turned into the position of attention. The three inspectors found themselves standing in broad daylight, amid the trees, flowers, and shrubbery of a convent garden.

"Under cover of darkness," Blanc completed the story, "the smugglers carried their kegs down this path to the gate there, and so on to the shops of some of the less scrupulous wine merchants. Heaven and the Excise Department will bless Sister Marie Joseph."

Blanc sat in his office, staring straight ahead of him at the closed door, his fingers drumming impatiently on his desk. To his right the tricolored flag stood drooping in its stand; to his left the portrait of the Emperor scowled down at him from the wall. To anyone who knew the Chief Inspector, the tight lines of his mouth and the grim set of his face foreboded trouble. In fact, Blanc was not so much angry as sick at heart. His confidential files were being rifled, and one of his men was a traitor.

Who was behind it? Fouché? He doubted it very much. The Minister of Police would have no reason or need to do that. He could simply ask to see any of his files, and as for spying, Fouché had no reason to suspect him of anything. No, it had to be Dubois. The Prefect had already had him followed—until Blanc had put a stop to that! Now he had bribed one of his men, and Blanc had to know which one it was. Cartier and Coimbeau had been full of laughter this morning when they showed him "The Gallery." Could either of them be hypocrite enough to laugh and joke with a man he was betraying?

Spying and betrayal were almost a way of life in today's Europe. (Had it always been that way? he wondered.) What would Fouché or Talleyrand, or one of the Emperor's other ministers do if he discovered he was being spied upon? He knew the answer. He would ignore it and pretend he didn't know. More likely, he'd put his own spy in the other fellow's camp. Better still, he would get the same man to work for him, by offering him more money.

Yes, that was what Fouché or Talleyrand would do. The question was, what was Inspector Blanc going to do? He didn't give a damn what that thievish Briviste swine was up to, as long as it didn't involve him. Let him go on issuing his idiotic proclamations and sticking his nose up prostitutes' skirts and into his dirty books. As long as he kept it out of the Criminal Investigation Department! As for the traitor, Blanc knew he was incapable of rewarding treachery, except with dismissal.

But, God! he hoped it wasn't Cartier, or Dourouflé, or Morel, or Coimbeau, or Delmotte, or LaFarge, or even young Bastard. And if it was one of them. . . . In the game of chess, he sternly reminded himself, when one loses a man one goes on without him. The question now was to discover which man he must remove, be he bishop, rook, or knave.

He had an idea. It was an old trick, one used by the secret police in the days of the Monarchy, but it still worked. Perhaps it would work this time.

The man of the Rue Saint-Guillaume sat at his favorite table, sipping a brandy and reading the afternoon papers. Throughout the afternoon, various friends and business associates had come up to him, chatted awhile, and then gone off again. His interest in the police's investigation of the murders was mainly a matter of curiosity. There was no link between himself and the victims. He had never even met or spoken to any of them before. And even if that Chief Inspector of theirs —what was his name again?—somehow, miraculously, found a connection, he had no proof. And if he had proof, there was still nothing he could do about it.

No, he was safe. Absolutely safe. Of that he was certain. What was uncertain was his future, his own career. His money was running out, and he needed to work again. He would have to line up several engagements—which was, in fact, what he was in the process of doing, even though, to the casual observer, he seemed to be idling.

He owed his manservant money, and his landlord, and his tailor, and his coachman, not to mention several other people about town. In truth, his debts didn't really worry him. They were no more than any gentleman of proper standing accrued in the course of a tolerable existence. He knew that one good job would easily wipe those out. The task before him now was to get it. He was dissatisfied with the offers he had gotten. Indeed, he did need money, but there was no need to let the world at large know that, nor would it do to cheapen his reputation by working for smaller fees.

That business in the Rue Saint-Guillaume was a one-time affair, something he had never done before and would never do again. It had cost him dearly, and not only in money. But it had, in fact, cost him a great deal of money. Still, he had no regrets, and he was determined never to have any.

Regrets! he said to himself. What the devil difference does it make whether I have any regrets or not? They're dead, and that's that. God knows they deserved it, even if men have forgotten. They may have gotten on in the world, they may have attained respectability, but I could never forget. Nor will I ever forget.

The man of the Rue Saint-Guillaume sat looking off into the distance. His deep-set, penetrating eyes failed to see the people in the cafe all around him. Instead he saw seven victims, four men and three women, seated stiff and erect in a Paris drawing room.

"Pardon, sir."

"What? What is it?"

He looked up and saw Josef, his regular waiter, standing over him.

"The *Afternoon Observer* has just arrived, sir."

"Oh, thank you, Josef." He took the paper from the old man with a practiced smile.

"My pleasure, sir."

Yes, there it was at last. Right on page one: the story of the killings. He read the details eagerly, devouring every scrap of information, rereading parts of the article again and again. At last, he said to himself. At long last.

Blanc had paid one of his unexpected visits, this time to the prefecture of the Sixth Arrondissement. It seems there was quite a bit of activity going on at the time. A huge brute of a butcher, one Victor Célestins, had taken a meat cleaver to his wife, Germaine, and practically split her in half. He then sat down on a stool next to the blood-soaked body, the cleaver still in his hand, and waited quietly for the police. Her screams had brought in the neighbors, and when the police arrived on the scene they found him in the same position, sitting absolutely motionless. He went along with them to the prefecture as docile as a lamb.

He was seated now on the cot in the prefecture's only cell, his hands clasped together between his knees, his face expressionless and his eyes unseeing.

"He's been that way for two hours," Inspector Dossin said. "Lucky for us we had no other guests at the time, although he's given us no trouble."

"What was it all about?" Blanc asked.

Dossin shrugged his shoulders expressively. "What's it ever about when a man kills a woman, Chief Inspector? I sometimes think they're more trouble than they're worth, although I wouldn't want to have my missus hear me say that."

Blanc looked at the huge, hairy man seated in the cell, and wondered what thoughts were going through his mind now. Was he thinking about the way it had ended for the two of them, or about the beginning, when they had first met and loved and married?

> For contemplation he and valour form'd,
> For softness she and sweet attractive grace;
> He for God only, she for God in him. . . .

"You're Inspector Blanc, aren't you? I've seen you before."

Blanc went over to the bars of the cell. "Yes, I'm Chief Inspector Blanc."

"Do you think they'll give me the guillotine for this?" The big man had gotten up and come close to the bars. He and the Chief Inspector were separated by only a few millimeters, each looking directly into the other's eyes.

"They might," Blanc replied, "or you might be put into an asylum, if your lawyer pleads insanity. You could get a long prison sentence, and then again, if it were a crime of passion, you could be freed. There are a number of possibilities."

"They can guillotine me. I don't give a damn."

"Why did you kill your wife, M. Célestins?"

There was a long pause while the man's broad peasant face displayed an obvious attempt to think, to explain his actions to himself.

"Germaine and I were married fourteen years. She was my woman. She was unfaithful to me, so I killed her."

As simple and direct as that, Blanc thought. And it happened among the upper classes, the aristocracy, and the monied bourgeoisie as readily as it did among the workers and peasants.

"You're still young enough to survive a prison sentence," he told the huge butcher. "If your lawyer pleads a crime of passion, and the jury agrees with him, you could walk out of this a free man."

The big man shook his head. "I don't want to go on without Germaine. They can guillotine me."

He sat back down on the cot and resumed the position he'd held before, staring off into nothingness.

"Did you know this Germaine?" Blanc asked Inspector Dossin.

"I did, Chief Inspector. A thin, frail little thing. Nothing to get excited about."

"Was she unfaithful to him?"

"I asked one of the neighbors that. She told me she was."

Blanc nodded. It was impossible for the casual observer to tell what was running through his mind. "Had they any children?"

"No, Chief Inspector."

"That's one fortunate thing. I don't think Célestins will put up much of a defense. He'll agree to anything the *juge d'instruction* says. Unless he changes his mind—and I don't think he will—he won't let his lawyer plead crime of passion." He took out his watch suddenly and looked at it. "*Au 'voir,* Dossin."

"*À bientôt,* Chief Inspector."

Seated in his coach on the way back to his office, Blanc

couldn't help thinking about the hairy giant in the cell and the fragile little woman he'd loved and murdered. If a neighbor knew about the wife's infidelity, that meant everyone had probably known—except the husband, of course. And when he finally found out, he killed her.

Wouldn't it have been better, he mused, if Célestins had kept his knowledge to himself and never let on? He and Germaine would still be living together, and the chances were that the affair would gradually have died out. Blanc's brain told him how ridiculous that was. He knew his man, and Célestins had no more chance of pretending ignorance and keeping his passions in check than a dark storm cloud has of not bursting.

Or, for that matter, than he himself had of not dealing with the man in his department whom he felt he could no longer trust. The only difference between Victor Célestins and myself, he said, is that I considered the alternative, whereas for him no other possibility ever existed. If there is such a thing as guilt or innocence, I am far more guilty than he.

His waiting room was empty. He asked the guard, Métons, whether any of his inspectors had been there in his absence. He named each one of them by name.

"No, Chief Inspector."

"You're certain, Métons."

"Absolutely, Chief Inspector."

Blanc went into his private office, shutting the heavy oak door behind him. Métons, my rascally young friend, I wonder whether you're aware that you've just sealed your own fate—and with one hair. He went over to his desk and saw that the hair he'd strung, just before going out, across the drawer where he kept his confidential files was broken. He felt frankly guilty about his sense of relief. But the obviousness of the choice hit him full in the face. Of course, Métons was the person in all of Paris with the easiest access to his office. He brought in the daily reports and placed them on his desk, whether he was in or not, brought in each of the papers as it arrived at the prefecture, and sometimes even brought in meals when he ate at his desk and took away the empty dishes afterward.

If Dubois had approached the wrong man, that worthy

would, in all probability, have reported the bribe attempt to his Chief. But the Prefect had an innate craftiness (the only thing Blanc would ever credit him with), the sure instinct that leads a thief to recognize another thief. He rang the cord that summoned the guard, and then sat down behind his desk. When the young man came in, he looked up and regarded him coldly.

"How much did Prefect Dubois pay you to steal my confidential files and let him read them? If you lie to me, Métons, you'll only make things worse for yourself."

If Métons had been perspiring in the Prefect's office the week before, he was positively melting now. The sweat ran down his face in rivulets.

"Inspector Blanc, I—"

"Stand at attention."

"Sir, I didn't think . . . I didn't mean—"

"Answer my question."

Métons took a deep breath. The sweat continued to pour down his face. "Five hundred francs."

"Altogether, or each time?"

Another pause, while the guard gasped for breath. "Each time, sir."

"How many times?"

"Four. . . . Only four, sir."

"When? The dates!"

"The first time . . . was about four months ago . . . May sixth, I think. . . ."

That was the time of the Besancourt affair, in which Dubois was directly involved.

". . . And again on May twenty-ninth. . . ."

No doubt Dubois had wanted to find out how much he had on him.

". . . Last Thursday . . . and again today."

But why now? What was he working on that could possibly interest the King of Thieves? "Did Prefect Dubois ask you about any of my cases?"

"Yes, sir. He mentioned that business about the seven corpses."

"The Rue Saint-Guillaume murders? What were his exact words?"

Métons hesitated for a moment. "He said— the Prefect said, 'I want those files about the seven people who were murdered, and that prisoner they've got.' He also asked me if you were working on any other case right now."

The scorpion stings because it cannot help but sting. The thief steals not because he covets the object but because he cannot help but steal. He pushed a pen and an inkwell across his desk and placed several pages of writing paper next to them.

"Sit down, Métons, and write out exactly what you have just told me. Then, at the bottom of your confession, state your request to resign from the Guardians of the Peace. It would also be to your advantage if you returned the money Prefect Dubois gave you. It will go to the widows of policemen who were killed in the line of duty."

Métons, who had already sat and begun writing, looked across the desk at the Chief Inspector. "I don't have the money any more. I bought things. I mean, except for today: I wasn't paid yet."

"Then, bring in the things you bought."

Métons wrote out his confession-resignation and affixed his name to it. Blanc read it over and noted that the young man's spelling and grammar could do with a bit of work.

"You may consider your request to resign accepted. Now go home. Tomorrow morning bring in your uniform and everything you purchased with the money Prefect Dubois paid you."

"I bought clothes, sir."

"Then, we'll sell them or give them away to the poor."

Guardian Métons stood up, snapped to attention, and turned smartly around. The Chief Inspector was busily working on some papers and neither looked up nor noticed him leave the room.

CHAPTER 6

Blanc felt frankly relieved about the outcome of the affair, and frankly guilty about his relief. Would he have behaved the same way had it been Cartier, say, or Morel? Would he have taken into consideration their years of service, the dangers they'd faced, the experiences they'd shared? Socrates taught, know thyself, and he did know himself. He would have done the same thing to one of them, and grieved about it privately.

He knew the sobriquet he had among some quarters of the police (and elsewhere as well): *"le petit Robespierre."* This referred not to his size—for Robespierre had been a small man, and probably shorter than himself—but his reputation for unyieldingness and incorruptibility. It wasn't a distinction he had consciously sought for himself, but once he'd acquired it he guarded it jealously.

So, now it was time to deal with that *souteneur* on the second floor. He had no illusions about getting Dubois dismissed, but by all the heavens he would make him sweat! He'd raised an unholy row the last time, when he discovered one of Dubois's men following him, even though he knew full well that it wasn't at all unusual for one department to spy on another. This time he had a signed confession, and he intended to make the most of it. No doubt the Prefect would find, in the labyrinthine sewers of his own mind, another way to keep a watch on him.

He marched up the stairs, stormed through the Prefect's waiting room, and opened his door without knocking. There he found Dubois in conference with Inspector Desny, another man for whom he felt the greatest contempt. The Prefect looked up in genuine surprise at the Chief Inspector, and surely couldn't miss the thunderclouds that hovered directly over his head.

"You'd better send your man outside, Dubois, unless of course you're afraid to be alone in the same room with me."

"What the devil do you mean—" Dubois sputtered.

"What the devil do you mean, bribing a man to steal my papers?"

"Desny, you'd better wait outside. I think our Chief Inspector has overstepped himself."

"Not *your* Chief Inspector, Dubois. I keep my hands in my own pockets."

Inspector Desny beat a hasty retreat. No doubt he'd keep his ears glued to the doors, though very little sound would penetrate through those massive oak portals.

"Have you forgotten, Blanc, that technically I'm your superior?"

"It was decided a long time ago that I was to report directly to the Minister of Police and to no one else. It was also agreed that there was to be no interference by you in my department."

He waved Métons's confession in the air and then shoved it directly under Dubois's nose. The Prefect read it and then looked up.

"What of it? This man isn't a member of your department. He's a policeman assigned as a guard to the prefecture."

"This man is no longer anything. He's resigned." Blanc snatched the paper out of the Prefect's hands. "Now I see why you keep Desny on: You need someone to read things to you."

"You've always been impertinent, Blanc. Now you're insulting. I haven't forgotten the allegation you made before in front of a witness, Inspector Desny."

"Don't try to change the subject. You bribed a man to steal confidential files from my desk, to bring them to you, and then to return them to me surreptitiously. The word, Dubois, means by stealth or without proper authority."

The other stood up. "You are talking to the Emperor's Prefect of Police. I find your manner rude and insulting, and your effrontery insufferable."

"And I find your bribery and corruption insufferable. But then, we're not telling each other anything new, are we?"

Dubois was obviously trying to maintain his dignity. "I gave a policeman orders. He obeyed those orders."

"*Merde!* No proper orders need to be reinforced by a bribe. You really do need to have things spelled out for you, don't you? And you're even wrong about the man's status. He was assigned to my department. Dubois, let me make this so plain that even you can't mistake me: If you ever try to bribe one of my men again, or interfere in my department or with my work, I'll drag you out into the middle of the street and horsewhip you."

Blanc turned on his heels and marched out of the Prefect's office. When he opened the doors, Inspector Desny jumped back several paces and tried mightily to appear nonchalant.

Michelle Desmans did more than brood around the house and read Goethe. She busied herself with household chores, supervised the shopping for and preparation of food, and resumed her embroidery. After the initial shock of their parents' murder, her brother had returned to their father's office (it was now Georges's office, but she still thought of it that way), and spent most of his days at the lawcourts. She was therefore left pretty much to her own devices and occupied herself as best she could.

Thus she found herself in the library dusting off her father's lawbooks, not because they were really dusty—Thérèse took care of that—but more to give herself something to do. She took each book off the shelf and dusted it separately (something Thérèse didn't do), hardly paying attention to their titles or their contents.

While her hands were thus engaged, her mind was wandering in another realm. Suddenly a sheet of paper dropped out of the book she was holding and fell onto the floor. She stooped to pick it up, and recognized the expensive foolscap her father had used for his letters. It was indeed a letter, written in her father's small, neat, and precise hand. But when she saw the name of the person to whom it was addressed, her heart began beating furiously.

Paris
28 Prairial IX

My Dear Pardon,

We had some harsh words the other night, and perhaps each of us said things we might in the future have cause to regret. You hurled a number of accusations at me and called me several names which I will not now bother to repeat. When I reminded you that, if I was guilty you were equally guilty, and that each of your epithets applied as well to yourself, you couldn't in truth deny my assertion.

You were furious with me because I told you then—as I do now—that I feel no guilt whatever. If you want to castigate yourself with outcries of *mea culpa,* that is of course your business, although I would not advise such a procedure. It can help no one at this point, and may do a great deal of harm. Think about that. Remember also that not only were we not condemned for our behavior: Quite the contrary, we were commended and rewarded. Therefore, what sort of "crimes" did we commit?

You asked me—rhetorically, I suppose—how history would judge us. I tell you frankly that I have no idea. I do maintain that, in the light of events as they were *then,* our actions were wholly justified. Strong measures were needed, and we took strong measures. We were empowered by the law, as the law then existed, and we did not exceed our authority.

In answer to another of your rhetorical questions—no, I do not boast about what we did. It is over and done with, and what is the point in bringing it up at all now? We did what we felt needed to be done. It is finished. It all lies in the past. Times change, attitudes change, laws change. No one who was not there, who was not involved and in the center of things, could be expected to understand. You of all people should realize that.

I shall not be seeing you before your departure. Whether we see each other when next you return to Paris will depend on you. In any event, do extend my regards to Mme. Pardon, and those of my wife as well.

I remain

The letter was unsigned. Michelle was so excited she wanted to send Thérèse immediately to the lawcourts to fetch her brother. But then she thought better of it. Georges would be unnecessarily alarmed, and she supposed the matter could, after all, wait till this evening. Nevertheless, she was in a state of high excitement all afternoon, something her maid couldn't fail to notice.

Normally Georges liked to stop off at a café near the Palais de Justice (as their father had done for years), a place frequented by lawyers. Since the tragedy, however, he hurried straight home from work, in order not to leave her alone any more than was necessary. Over dinner they would exchange gossip about the day's events, discuss their plans for the coming season, or talk about their brother, Philippe. Afterward he would work at his writing table while she quietly sat reading a book, each warmed by the other's presence.

On this day, though, she ran to the door as soon as she heard his footsteps, threw her arms around his neck, and practically dragged him into the library. Georges Desmans asked his sister to leave him alone while he studied the document, and even took the precaution of locking the library doors after her.

He did some fast mental computation and translated the date—from that barbaric Revolutionary calendar—to June 19, 1801. A day or two either way would hardly matter. He read the letter through twice, and then put it down on the desk. As it was found here and not among M. Pardon's documents, one of two possibilities suggested itself. It was either a draft for a letter his father had written to M. Pardon (and he knew his father as a precise, cautious man who did make first drafts of his letters), or it was the letter itself and had never been sent.

He noted wryly that his father had been careful never to state precisely what the matter was that had been the cause of disagreement between himself and his former friend. He had not the slightest doubt that this was no mere accident of omission, but a precaution lest the letter (or draft) ever fall into the wrong hands.

Still, he had done some probing on his own into his father's past, even before the tragedy, and he had a reasonably good idea of what "actions" the letter referred to. The question that bothered him was whether the letter had been sent. And if so, had M. Pardon destroyed it—torn it up in a fit of rage—or had it been found by Inspector Blanc among Pardon's documents?

Blanc had gone through all of his father's documents, in his presence, both here and at the office, and had never made mention of such a note. Therefore Georges tended to doubt that another copy (if there was one) had survived.

So be it! If Blanc had the letter, he had it. There was nothing he could do about that. But if not. . . .

"What is the point in bringing it up at all now?" The phrase from his father's letter ran through his mind. "It is finished. It all lies in the past." The police had their man—or thought they did, which amounted to the same thing. The case was as good as closed. "It can help no one at this point, and may do a great deal of harm."

It wasn't really a cold day. Brisk would be a better word for it. Still, there was a bit of premature chill in the air, and it wouldn't seem too unreasonable to light a fire. He went over to the fireplace. As soon as he had a respectable blaze going, he threw in the letter and stood by until it was entirely consumed. Rubbing his hands briskly, he went to the library doors and opened them.

"I'm chilled. It's cool out today. And I'm famished. What do we have for dinner, Michou?"

On their way in to the dining room he said, quite casually, "I have to be at the Palais de Justice tomorrow, and it's right near the Prefecture. I'll drop off the letter on my way."

Blanc knew the day of reckoning was at hand, and it came on the very following day. *Dies irae. Dies illa.* The penalty we pay for telling the truth here on earth. He found a note on his desk in the morning asking him to call at the Ministry of Police. He might as well get it over with. He smiled grimly at his anticipation of Fouché taking the title of the Paris Police quite literally, and appointing himself as keeper of the peace. Or rather, its restorer.

He threw on his cape and ran hastily across the street through the rain. The Minister's waiting room was empty, and he knocked on the heavy oak door. Devereaux opened the door, held it open for him, and then let himself out, closing the door behind him.

"Sit down, Blanc."

No good morning.

The Minister came straight to the point. "I hear there was quite an altercation between you and Prefect Dubois yesterday afternoon. He tells me you threatened him with physical violence in front of one of his inspectors."

"That's not quite correct, M. le Ministre. I called him dishonest in front of one of his inspectors. I made the threat to horsewhip him in private. What's more," the Chief Inspector added, "I meant it."

Fouché shook his head incredulously. "Blanc, Blanc. Wouldn't it have been enough just to lodge a protest? Why this great pretense of surprise at something you know goes on all the time?"

"It doesn't go on in my department. I want Dubois to keep his sticky fingers out of my department and off my men."

"Are you afraid he'll corrupt them? You know that no one can be corrupted unless he wants to be. In fact," the Minister observed, "our Prefect was doing you a favor. He was testing your men for you. You should have let him go on, and then you'd have known exactly which of them could be touched and which ones couldn't."

"I'd hate to think of Prefect Dubois as the barometer of the French Empire."

"Nevertheless, he is the Prefect, and your handling of the matter was hardly subtle."

"No," Blanc agreed, "it wasn't."

"What you said to him in private isn't all that important. But you admit you accused him of dishonesty in front of another inspector."

"If Prefect Dubois wishes to make an issue of that, I will produce witnesses."

The Minister raised his eyebrows.

"I'll bring in a dozen girls off the streets who will testify that they pay a private 'tax' to our Prefect."

"I wouldn't permit it."

"Then, don't permit him to make an issue of it."

"I have no intention of letting an issue arise out of a momentary flare-up. As a matter of fact, Dubois wanted to challenge you to a duel. You find that amusing?"

"I find it hilarious. A duel in the Bois de Boulogne between the two most inept swordsmen in all Paris. On second thought, the Cirque would be a better place to stage it. Our citizens would gladly pay seven francs each for such a spectacle."

"He's not that bad a swordsman."

"In any case, the choice of weapons would be mine, and I'd choose pistols. I'm a fairly good shot."

"You won't get the chance to prove it. Not against Dubois, anyway."

"I was afraid not. Dubois reminds me of a bully we had in our village who would only threaten to fight when he knew there was someone around to hold him back. If he really wanted a duel, he'd have challenged me directly, without first telling you."

"I'd have found out anyway and put a stop to it. I'd have to. I cannot have the Paris police split up into two factions, two opposing armies, Blanc's men and Dubois's men."

"'The King's men and the Cardinal's men.'" Blanc quoted the once familiar phrases.

"Exactly."

There was a momentary pause as the two men regarded each other.

"I won't apologize," Blanc said.

"Oh, yes you will. Dubois will express his regrets for being overzealous in the pursuit of his duties. You will express yours for momentarily losing your temper."

"And then," Blanc added, "we both go dancing together at Tivoli."

Neither man could keep a straight face any longer. They both burst into laughter. The air was lightened, and they were able to resume their normal relationship.

"Now, more than ever before, the police need to hang together. The Emperor questioned me about the Rue Saint-Guillaume murders yesterday. He wanted to know whether I thought we really had our man."

Blanc looked keenly at his superior. "What did you tell him?"

"I told his Majesty that I felt there was enough evidence against Léon to get a conviction."

Once again Blanc marveled at the man's skill as a consummate diplomat. What Fouché had done was to tell the Emperor nothing more or less than the truth—without answering his question.

"The trouble is," Fouché went on, "I can't hold out much longer. The Emperor, the press, and the public will be clamoring for a trial. How far have you gotten on the case?"

"I will go you one better, M. le Ministre. I will tell you the truth and answer your question fully. I have gotten nowhere."

The Minister reflected for a few moments before replying. He played with one of the quill pens on his desk.

"Since you've become Chief of the Criminal Investigation Department there have been only three unsolved crimes in Paris. Yet all that will be forgotten if you let Léon go. And the ironic thing is that the cloud of suspicion would hang over his head the rest of his life anyway. Most people would still be convinced he was guilty."

"But I know he's innocent. And so do you."

Fouché emitted a sigh from somewhere deep inside his massive chest. "If he were an honest citizen I could understand this passion of yours for justice."

"Sometimes the principle is bigger than the man. We've still got time. The case is only two weeks old."

"Do you have any idea of who might have killed them?"

"No."

"Have you any theories about how he managed it?"

"No."

"Do you know why he did it?"

"Yes."

For the second time that morning the Minister raised his eyebrows.

"I found the connection between the four men." Blanc explained the relationship between the four in detail.

"Well," Fouché remarked, his spirits noticeably rising, "that narrows the field of suspects down to a mere eighty thousand. In fact, as we are both agreed the murderer was a man, we can cut that number down to a paltry forty thousand—every one of whom had a motive."

"In fact, we can cut the field of suspects down to one. The

crime is indeed unique in my experience, but it is in that very uniqueness that the murderer gave himself away. There is only one man in the entire world who has the ability to do what he did. Now we know where he's from and why he did it."

Fouché looked steadily into his subordinate's eyes. Then he nodded his head slightly. "You're right. I think we can hold on a bit longer."

Blanc left the prefecture early to go home to wash up and change into civilian clothing. By the time he left his house, the heavy rains had abated and the day had turned into a cool, clouded, and windswept evening. Yet it was not at all an unpleasant night. The weather mattered hardly at all to him; he would have braved the fires of hell or the ice of Greenland for this evening. He would have endured fire, earth, air, and water—and he wasn't even a Freemason. He was grateful that nothing had come up to call him away. Not even a fresh development in his case!

He picked up Daphne at her home, and they hurried on in his coach to the Théâtre des Italiens. He was also grateful that she was free this evening and able to come with him. Daphne Perrault was wearing a magnificent gown of sapphire-blue velvet that displayed her superb shoulders. Fastened over those shoulders now was a white moiré cape, the whole of it created by Auguste Garneray, Leroy's official designer.

There would be a brilliant audience assembled tonight: marshals, dukes, bankers, diplomats, all dressed to the nines, with their ladies showing off their dresses by Bertin, Rimbault, Garneray, and Leroy himself. None of it mattered to Blanc. He felt that this evening had been organized for him and him alone.

The Théâtre des Italiens, in association with the Comédie Française, was presenting the first Paris performance of Mozart's *Don Giovanni* in the original Italian. The best musician in Paris, Spontini, was the *chef d'orchestre,* and Benoist, of the Comédie, was the director. The singers, Elleviou, Martin, Armand, Garat, Grassini, headed the best cast that could be assembled. In fact, there had been a performance a few years earlier, with the opera drastically rewritten and the addition of several new characters not envisaged by Mozart or Da Ponte.

Tonight's performance, however, was complete and authentic, even including the additions Mozart had made for the Vienna premiere.

From an architectural standpoint alone, the Italiens was Blanc's favorite theater. From the street it looked like a Grecian temple, pure and simple in its chaste beauty, unadulterated by the Roman elaboration of the Greek style, or the French embellishments of the Roman.

The Boulevard des Italiens was lined with coaches. Liveried attendants helped the ladies alight as the caravan moved on, its vehicles having discharged their distinguished occupants.

As they entered the crowded foyer, Daphne realized that Blanc was inhabiting a world of his own. Perhaps he was in Prague with Mozart, Da Ponte, and Casanova as they put the finishing touches on their *opera buffa*. She smiled (a charming smile the gentlemen around her couldn't fail to notice). She could understand to some degree how he felt: If a play by Molière or Racine were being given for the first time—in its original, unbastardized form—she, too, would be ecstatic.

An attendant led them to their seats in the parquet circle. The orchestra players were already in their places. The performance was due to start promptly at seven and, at seven precisely, Spontini made his entrance, greeted by a wave of applause. Using his hands instead of the traditional violin bow, he extended his arms as a total hush enveloped the packed house.

Then he brought down his right arm, and the first, ominous chords of the overture rang out. Blanc was indeed transported to another world. Never in his life had he heard such beauty, but it was beauty with terror in it. Then the slowly syncopated measures, still darkly colored. Now a simple scale with a large crescendo—but what an effect! What a strange sense of uneasiness in what purported to be a comedy! The introduction over with, the music now became truly Mozartean, gay and witty. There was no formal ending to the overture. It simply dissolved into the opening scene and Leporello's complaints, to a lumbering rhythm, about being the underpaid, overworked servant of a hard master.

Blanc's only knowledge of Italian was through the years of

Latin he had studied under old Père Durand in the Auvergne, and much of the rapid-fire *recitativo* of the work was lost on him. But he was able to understand quite clearly the words in the long-flowing arias. And when Leporello began his patter song, *Madamina, il catalogo,* Blanc realized he was listening to the greatest comic air ever written.

Even the intermission, with everyone milling around the foyer and Daphne hanging on his arm and greeting all and sundry, didn't break the spell for Blanc.

They were back in their seats now as the curtain rose on the second act. A square in Seville before Donna Elvira's house. Don Giovanni has his fickle heart set on Elvira's pretty servant girl and gets Leporello to trick Elvira into leaving with him by exchanging cloaks with his servant. . . .

In the final scene, when the stone guest comes to keep the Don's invitation, there was again the same music as at the beginning of the overture. The statue gives the libertine one last chance to repent, but the proud nobleman refuses, as flames rise up all around him and an offstage chorus announces his eternal damnation. . . .

The audience's enthusiasm knew no bounds. One curtain call after another. People threw flowers. Only one man was not there to acknowledge the cheers: the composer, who had died nineteen years before in Vienna at the age of thirty-six, and whose corpse had been thrown into an unmarked pauper's grave.

The opera was a long one, although it didn't seem so, and ended too late for them to go to a restaurant. Blanc and Daphne returned to her house on the Rue Saint-Honoré for a cold supper.

"Beautiful as it was, I thought the Epilogue was an anticlimax, didn't you?" Daphne asked.

"It's a matter of taste," Blanc replied, "and evidently the composer himself was undecided about it. He wrote the Epilogue for the premiere in Prague and dropped it at the first Viennese performance, a year later."

"How do you feel about it?"

"I like it. But then, I adore every note Mozart ever wrote. Actually, this version of the Don Juan legend follows not Molière's play but the old Spanish street performances, which always had an epilogue with a moral."

"You're so knowledgeable," Daphne said, half jokingly and half sincerely.

Blanc shrugged his shoulders modestly. "One can't chase criminals all the time."

"You know, I'm surprised M. and Mme. de Luynes weren't there tonight. I looked for them."

"The Italiens isn't a large theater," Blanc replied. "It's not considered as 'prestigious' as the Opéra, although personally I prefer it, thanks mainly to Spontini."

"But they like music—the De Luynes, I mean. I saw her last week, but I forgot to ask her whether they were going tonight. Incidentally, you were wrong about Mme. de Luynes's reception. She did want you there. She told me last week that she specifically wanted you as a keen observer and an impartial witness. She had Berini as her special guest that evening. You know, that extraordinary man all Paris society has been talking about. They say he studied with Mesmer in Vienna, and he's able to put a whole roomful of people into a trance."

For a brief moment Blanc forgot his manners. "What?" he said. "What was that?"

CHAPTER 7

To say that the prefecture was alert the following morning would be an understatement. The place was electrified. Cartier, Morel, Dourouflé, Coimbeau, Delmotte, and LaFarge had all been brought together again. Then they had been sent out to comb all of Paris for the Murderer of Rue Saint-Guillaume, whose name they now knew and whose place of origin and motive Blanc now knew. The first policeman to become involved in this case—other than the young *gardien*—Inspector Richard, was already out on the hunt. Shortly afterward, Terrell and young Bastard were added to the hunt party.

Despite his excitement (and lack of sleep), Blanc couldn't help being amused by the sight of Terrell and Bastard together as he briefed them in his office. The sad-eyed, long-faced Terrell always reminded him of a basset hound. Bastard, on the other hand, eager to please and anxious to prove himself, brought to his mind a frisky terrier. Indeed, this was going to be quite a hunt!

Lugubrious and taciturn he might well be, but Blanc knew Terrell as a devoted and reliable inspector. As for young Bastard, he had not yet proved himself, but he needed to be given a chance. It was just possible that he might get one this time.

And what kind of animal, he wondered, was this man Berini? For that matter, what sort of animal are you, Inspector Blanc? He liked to think of himself as a bloodhound, of course, especially at times like these, but he knew there were people who thought of him as a member of another species. A fox, perhaps, or a hawk, or even a rat.

Eager as he was to capture the Murderer of Rue Saint-Guillaume, the man who called himself Berini, Blanc was nevertheless glad that Daphne hadn't made her memorable remark before the performance last night, or at the intermission. To have torn himself away from an event that he considered one of the highlights of his life would have caused him immeasurable grief. Even the arrest of the killer wouldn't have compensated for that!

He had left Daphne with a hasty explanation and gone straight over to Fouché's residence on the Rue le Regrattier. He knew the Minister probably wouldn't be asleep, and even if he was he wouldn't mind being awakened for a development like this. Besides, he needed information, and whom better to get it from than the man who reputedly knew everyone and everything in Paris. Blanc had never heard of Berini, but then, he'd been away from Paris for several weeks and had, in fact, only returned two days before the murders. Also, he was not a member of the *haut monde* and wasn't generally invited to the fashionable salons.

Fouché was at work in his study, and Blanc was immediately admitted to his presence. The Minister wore a silk dressing gown and was studying several documents at his desk. Like Blanc, he preferred working by candlelight rather than the more prevalent oil lamps.

"Berini," the Minister said. "I know about him, of course, but I haven't attended any of his demonstrations. I understand the man is Swiss, that he studied with Mesmer in Vienna, and that he's performed in Paris before. I know he's been invited to the best salons—no doubt for a healthy fee—to demonstrate the science of . . . let me see, what is it called again?" He searched his memory for a few moments. "Animal magnetism. Yes, that's it. Animal magnetism."

In fact, Blanc had remembered the phrase back in Daphne's drawing room. As soon as she mentioned the name of the Viennese physician, something came alight in his brain. Still, he tactfully refrained from prompting the Minister. *Animal magnetism.*

"I don't pretend to understand the theory," Fouché went on, "but evidently Mesmer possessed the power, and he passed it on to this man Berini. Well, Blanc, I confess you've really caught me out this time. I should have thought of Berini at once. I didn't."

He spread his hands out in a small deprecating gesture. It was the first time in their long relationship that Blanc had ever heard him admit to a mistake or a failing. He said nothing.

"But why should a Swiss mystifier murder seven people against whom he had no personal vendetta? Unless he only put them to sleep, and then someone else did the killing."

Blanc shook his head. "No. Berini was the sixth guest in that house and the only other person in that room. And he's no more Swiss than I am."

"You're probably right," Fouché agreed. "You've been right about everything else so far. By the way, how was the performance this evening?"

Catching Blanc's surprised look, the Minister laughed. "Don't worry, my friend, I haven't pulled a Dubois on you. Give me credit for some powers of observation. From the way you're dressed you've obviously been out, and there's only one place in Paris where you would have been tonight."

Blanc had forgotten he was wearing his dress clothes. "It was magnificent," he said. "Even that much abused word 'masterpiece' is inadequate to describe this work. But if tonight's reception is any indication, the opera ought to be playing for weeks. You ought to go see it."

"I will. And I have no doubt you'll return there yourself. That is, after you've caught Berini and have the leisure to do so. Well, Chief Inspector, your evening ended quite differently from the way it began, didn't it? Two different worlds: Mozart and the Murderer of Rue Saint-Guillaume."

"Not all that different, M. le Ministre," Blanc said. "In fact, all the pieces are starting to come together. The circle is closing. Mozart performed before Dr. Mesmer in Vienna when he was a boy."

Blanc next called upon Inspector Richard, whose address he had gotten from Fouché. He had also asked the Minister where Berini was staying, but that information Fouché was unable to give him. At least, not there, in his house. It was agreed that Blanc was to pick up Richard and that the two of them would meet Fouché at the Ministry.

Honoré Richard lived with his wife and two children in a

modest apartment on the Rue Beau-repaire. Mme. Richard, who answered the door, was a pleasant, modest-looking woman who seemed completely overawed by her soldierly husband. She reminded Blanc, in her total self-effacement, of the typical army wife of every officer who has not made general.

Richard himself came into the drawing room, where Mme. Richard had led Blanc, wearing an old worn robe over his night shirt. Nevertheless, he still carried himself with perfect military bearing. His wife retired from the room, presumably to return to their bedchamber.

"I'm sorry to get you up at this hour, Richard, but we've got a break in the Rue Saint-Guillaume murders. I thought you'd want to be in on this."

Richard's normally stern face broke into a grin. "Thanks, Chief. You know I'd have felt offended if you'd left me out. The one thing I'm dying to know is how he did it."

"Get dressed," Blanc said, "and I'll tell you about it on our way to the Ministry."

While Richard was dressing, Blanc stood in the middle of the room, balancing lightly on the balls of his feet. He knew perfectly well how Richard felt, and he himself loved this sort of thing: chasing around Paris in the middle of the night.

Once an investigation broke, and he and his department were able to swing into action, he was the happiest man alive. Daphne, Paris, Mozart, and a criminal hunt. Give him these and he was content. And to have all of them in one night was almost too good to be true.

He also realized, as he had sensed from the very beginning, that he was faced here with a worthy adversary. For the first time in a long while, he had an opponent who really posed a challenge to his mental faculties. Instead of a ridiculous duel with that idiot Dubois, here was a contest between two equals. He frankly didn't expect Berini to be in Paris any longer, but he had, as a matter of course, to comb the entire city.

Richard came back into the room, dressed in his powder blue *gardien's* uniform with the gold braid that inspectors wore, his boots highly polished (by Mme. Richard, no doubt), his tricorne already on his head. He looked better in uniform than any other policeman Blanc knew.

"You said to the Ministry, Chief—"

"To the Ministry, Richard. *En avant.*"

Every foreigner who visited France had to register with the police. For that matter, every Frenchman who came to Paris was supposed to do that, but the police knew perfectly well that that law was often circumvented. The Ninth Arrondissement was filled with people living in small pockets who hadn't bothered to register, some through ignorance, others through fear.

If they were discovered but were nevertheless law-abiding, they generally managed to get off with a reprimand and a belated chance to register. If their occupations were of a questionable nature, they were unceremoniously escorted out of the city (often after a night in jail) and told to go back to their own towns or villages.

It was nearly 3:00 A.M. when Richard and Blanc arrived at the Ministry, the latter still wearing his fine dress clothes. Fouché was waiting for them in his office, where he had Berini's registry ready for them. The Minister's office was lit by candlelight, and the effect, with its play of lights and shadows, made the chamber quite different from what it was in the daytime. Instead of an official government bureau, it gave the room and its occupants a fine conspiratorial air. Blanc knew Fouché as a man who functioned well in the middle of the night. Evidently, Richard was another. That made three of them.

Fouché handed Blanc the registry card, and the Chief Inspector read it aloud. "Berini. (No Christian name.) Place of birth, Geneva. Home, 27 Avenue Descartes, Geneva. Residence in Paris, Hotel Baudoins in the Carrousel, where arrived on July 21 with coachman, Charles Steiner."

Another thing Blanc realized was that Fouché was under no illusions that Berini was still in Paris. Neither, probably, was Richard. Nevertheless, it was to the new Hotel Baudoins that the two inspectors repaired. The old porter, Maurice, whom Blanc knew, went to fetch the landlord, M. Roncard.

"Ah, yes, Berini." Roncard had taken them into his own room, which also served as his office. "Quite an extraordinary gentleman. He stayed with us for several weeks, from July twenty-first until—" he consulted his registry—"until September tenth."

Blanc and Richard looked at each other. The day the murders were committed.

"At what time did Berini leave this hotel?"

"As I recall, he left in a most unusual manner. Oh, he paid his bill all right, but he didn't leave here officially. He just handed the porter a bag of louis—enough to cover his charges here—and went off in his carriage."

"Why didn't you notify the police that he had gone?"

"He paid his bill. . . ."

"At what time did he leave here?"

"The porter who is on duty in the daytime would know that. That's Édouard."

"Does he sleep here?"

"No, Chief Inspector. He lives at home with his wife and four children. Will I get into trouble for failing to notify the police of a guest's departure?"

Would it really have mattered if Roncard had informed his local prefecture of Berini's sudden flight? It would have been duly noted somewhere, and no one—least of all Blanc himself—would have been able to put two and two together in time to intercept him.

"No," Blanc replied. "Just don't forget next time. Where does Édouard live?"

"On the Rue du Petit Muse."

"Send someone to fetch him immediately."

M. Roncard was about to ask whether the matter couldn't wait till morning, but as he opened his mouth he realized he had already jeopardized his good standing with the police through his oversight. Besides, two inspectors, one of them the Chief of the Criminal Investigation Department, would hardly be here at this hour of the night if it weren't important. What he said instead was "Of course, Chief Inspector. I'll see to it immediately. Excuse me a moment."

He stepped outside to give his instructions to Maurice. Then he came back into the room. "Maurice has gone to get

Édouard. I'm sure he'll be here as quickly as he can. In the meantime, may I offer you gentlemen something?"

Wasn't it the Emperor himself who had made the remark about "two-o'clock courage"? Blanc didn't feel the need for much courage at the moment, but he could certainly use something to brace himself. Ideally, it ought to go with strong black coffee.

"Coffee and a brandy would be fine," he suggested, "if we could get coffee at this hour."

Monsieur Roncard drew himself up to his full height, which, at 157 centimeters, wasn't terribly impressive.

"Gentlemen," he said, "this is the Hotel Baudoins. Here everything is possible."

In fact, it took over an hour for Maurice to arrive back at the hotel with Édouard, by which time dawn had broken and Blanc, Richard, and M. Roncard had consumed an entire pot of coffee and several glasses of Charentes cognac. Blanc couldn't help smiling at the memory of "The Gallery," the house at the Passy barrier, and the cellar of the Convent of the Filles-Sainte-Marie that the aroma of the brandy brought back.

Roncard had ventured earlier that he hoped M. Berini wasn't in any trouble ("such a fine gentleman"), but when the Chief Inspector ignored his question, he dropped the matter and didn't bring it up again.

Like Maurice, the night porter, Édouard had been in service with M. Roncard for many years. His reply to Blanc's question wasn't precise, but it was close enough to satisfy the two inspectors. "Karl, M. Berini's coachman, asked me to help him carry their trunks down. What time was that? Oh, I didn't look at a clock, Inspector Blanc. But I think it must have been sometime between three and four in the afternoon. I had no sooner finished helping Karl strap the last trunk onto the coach than M. Berini himself showed up. He told me they were in a hurry to leave, gave me something for myself, and handed me a bag of money that he said would take care of their expenses at the hotel. Then, without so much as a by-your-leave, he climbed into his coach and the two of them drove off."

Blanc arrived at the prefecture shortly before six. It was the beginning of what looked to be a fine, brisk, sunny autumnal day. He sent four policemen around to rouse his inspectors, to tell them to report directly to him instead of to their own arrondissements. He also sent Alphonse home to bring him a fresh uniform. Then he told his coachman he could return home and go to sleep. He himself would nap sometime during the day on a cot in his office. He had worked this way before.

And so the inspectors had been summoned, briefed, and dispatched to their various assignments. He had nine men working on this case. The nine best policemen in Paris. Probably the nine best policemen in the world. Ten, counting himself, and more likely than not Fouché would be involved directly again. Still, he couldn't help thinking of this case as a duel between himself and Berini. Did Berini even know of his existence? He honestly hoped not. He needed every advantage he could get, for Berini had the substantial advantage of a carefully formulated plan and a considerable head start.

His men, armed with a description of Berini that Blanc had gotten from M. Roncard and his employees, would conduct a thorough search of Paris, arrondissement by arrondissement, street by street, house by house. Only then, after he had gone over Paris with a fine-tooth comb, could he justify sending out messengers and emissaries to God knows where to track him down. In truth, he was already setting the wheels in motion for that purpose, under the quite valid assumption that Berini was no longer in Paris.

His uniform arrived. He went to the bathroom, washed, shaved, got dressed, and walked over to the Café Français for breakfast. He could have had something sent in to his office, but it was a beautiful day and, despite his lack of sleep (or perhaps because of it), he felt too exhilarated to stay indoors. Actually, the cafe generally first opened for lunch, but the *patron*, Freire, lived upstairs and could be counted on to get something together for you on short notice. Blanc, as well as some of the other inspectors, would go there in the morning if they had arrived early at the prefecture or had spent the night there.

Inevitably, M. Freire would come downstairs, greet his early visitor, and conduct him to a table. He would announce sol-

emnly that he would see what he could do. Then, just as inevitably, he would bring in hot coffee, a pitcher of cream, fresh
croissants, fruit, cheese, scrambled eggs, and a ham. It was a
splendid feast with which to start the day, or end it if you were
going home to bed.

Blanc had no intention of going to bed. He had already decided where his first call of the day would be. He'd decided
that last night at Daphne's house. Breakfast finished, a much
larger one than he normally ate at home (he always felt hun-
grier when he was without sleep), he went out into the bright
morning sunshine to find a cab. He walked the two streets over
to the Palais de Justice, whistling a tune he suddenly realized
was Don Giovanni's serenade.

The city that had been dead only a few hours before was
alert and bustling now. Judges, lawyers, policemen, clerks
were standing in front of the Palais de Justice, talking and ar-
guing. Each group formed its own circle, as it did every morning. Everyone there knew the Chief Inspector, and a number
of men greeted him as he walked past. He in turn raised the
tip of his forefinger to his tricorne in salutation. Those who
knew him better than merely by sight could usually tell, from
the way he did it, what sort of mood he was in that day. This
morning his greeting was positively jaunty.

He spotted a coachman he knew, Eugène, who had just
discharged his fare, a fat old lawyer named Procours, and
caught his eye.

"Where to, Inspector Blanc?"

"Three Rue Pierre."

He settled back in the carriage and enjoyed the morning, the
sunshine, and the busy crowds. Why, he wondered, was he so
happy? Berini had committed his crime and given them all the
slip. What's more, it was only a chance remark made by
Daphne that had given this case its new turn of events.

He was happy because he'd taken a big gamble—greater
than that of all the players at the gaming tables of the Palais-
Royal combined. And he'd won. Yet even if Daphne hadn't
said it then and there, he would have heard about Berini even-
tually. There was no question in his mind—or, more important,
in Fouché's now—who the Murderer of Rue Saint-Guillaume

was. His own faith and stubbornness in holding out under pressure had been justified. Even the police couldn't come out of this too badly: The murderer had fled Paris before the corpses were even discovered and reported. Yet, without a single witness, they had found him out.

And now the duel had begun. The duel between the mystifier who called himself Berini and who practiced animal magnetism, and the police inspector who used his wits, gambled with his career, and practiced the principles of Thomas Paine.

Number 3 Rue Pierre was another of those splendid houses owned by the people who made up the *haut monde* of Paris, those elegant, stylish, monied people who wielded the influence and power that determined the city's commerce, fashions, and culture. Some were mere pretenders, but Blanc had heard (from Daphne) that the De Luynes were the authentic article.

He handed the maid his card and was asked to wait in the hallway. It was a somewhat lengthy wait, and he could imagine Mme. de Luynes combing her hair, putting on makeup, and then donning her dressing robe to make herself presentable. When she came out, he saw that that was exactly what she had done. She was a small, thin woman, with a narrow face, bright, alert eyes, and graying hair, two ringlets of which she wore down the front of her shoulders. She wasn't attractive, but she probably spent a great deal of money on clothing and cosmetics.

"Chief Inspector Blanc," she said, in a not unmelodious voice, "Annie should have taken you into the drawing room. Please follow me."

The room itself was splendidly furnished, the predominant colors being blue and gold.

"You see," she said, indicating his uniform, "you fit in perfectly."

She sat down at a small *jardinière* and invited Blanc to take the chair opposite her.

"Would you like some coffee?"

"No, thank you, Madame. I've been drinking it all night."

"I shall have some, then.

"Annie!" she called out.

Her maid came in, curtsied, and left the room.

"How is Mlle. Perrault?"

"Fine, thank you. We went to the Théâtre des Italiens last night. In fact, she was expecting to see you there."

"Oh, yes, that thing by Mozart. Tell me, Inspector, do you really think Gluck and Mozart are as good as Lesueur and Martini? But I'm sorry. Of course you didn't come here this morning to chatter about music."

Blanc smiled. "Not exactly, Madame, but we can discuss music another time, if you like. What I did come for this morning was to chatter about animal magnetism."

Her eyes opened wide for just the tiniest fraction of a second and then returned to their normal look. One of the things the *haut monde* prided themselves on was never showing surprise at anything.

"I presume you're referring to Berini. Have you ever met the man?"

"No. Nor have I ever seen his demonstration. Tell me about him."

"Well, to begin with the man himself, he's arrogant, masterful, demanding—and devastatingly handsome. I'm sure no prima donna at the Opéra gives M. Devismes a more difficult time."

"Really? In what way?"

"Berini makes it clear at the outset that he doesn't present his scientific demonstrations before just anyone. His audiences are carefully selected for their knowledge and discernment. He even goes so far as to check the guest list with the hostess. Would you believe it, Chief Inspector! He must give his approval to your guests in your own house!"

"Why does the hostess put up with it, Madame? Why did you put up with it?"

"My dear, he's the rage of Paris. Why, no salon is worthy of attendance this season unless Berini has performed there."

Blanc was gaining an ever greater respect for his opponent.

"And then," Mme. de Luynes went on, "there are his eyes. The most beautiful, magnificent eyes I have ever seen in a man. You feel as if they could see into your very soul."

"Probably they can," Blanc commented. "Would you describe to me exactly how Berini conducts his performance, or demonstration?"

"The curtains are drawn. There is no light from outside, although the room is not in complete darkness. A few oil lamps are dimly lit. Everyone sits in a comfortable chair or couch facing Berini, who stands in front of the group at a table, upon which there is an oil lamp. He asks for a volunteer. Invariably, I understand, one of the ladies present is more than eager to oblige. Here in my house his first subject was Mme. Prescarts.

"He has the subject come up and stand in front of him. He asks her to free her mind of all thoughts, ideas, and associations. In Mme. Prescarts's case this initial request was hardly necessary. Then, after he has put the subject at her ease, he takes out a gold watch and holds it in front of her eyes in such a way that it reflects the light of the table lamp. He holds the watch by its chain, and lets it gently swing back and forth, like a pendulum. The subject follows the movement of the watch with her eyes, without moving her head.

"While he is doing this, Berini continues to talk. Softly, calmly, but with a definite note of authority in his voice, he tells the subject she will soon be fast asleep. I don't know how long it took Berini to put Mme. Prescarts to sleep. Sitting in half darkness, listening to a quiet voice drone on, seeing a flash of gold wave back and forth, one tends to lose track of time. Probably it was no more than a few minutes.

"Berini then turned Mme. Prescarts toward the rest of us, and there was no question about her being asleep. She doesn't have the intelligence to deceive anyone. However, Berini spoke to her and gave her instructions.

"'When I clap my hands three times,' he said, 'you will wake up, and you will remember nothing that happened.'"

"Excuse me," Blanc interrupted, "how many guests did you have?"

"Fourteen," she replied. "And, of course, my husband and myself."

"Please go on."

"Berini then led Mme. Prescarts back to her chair. She did indeed look like a sleepwalker. Then he said again, 'I will now clap my hands three times. On the third clap you will wake up. You will feel refreshed, in perfect health, and you will remember nothing.'

"On the third clap, Inspector Blanc, she did indeed wake up. She blinked, looked all around her, and then said triumphantly, 'There, you see, M. Berini, you weren't able to put me to sleep after all!'

"As you can imagine, the whole company shrieked with laughter.

"'And now,' Berini said, 'I should like to have one of the gentlemen volunteer.'

"There were a few moments of hesitation, and it was plain that the men were reluctant, and so my husband, as host, stood up and came forward. Again there was the swinging watch, and presently Gaston, my husband, was asleep. Berini then led him back to his chair, next to mine, and I tell you, Chief Inspector, that he definitely was asleep. After twenty-five years of marriage a woman knows whether her husband is feigning sleep or not.

"Berini then began giving my husband instructions and, fast asleep though he was, Gaston obeyed them.

"'You are driving a carriage, M. de Luynes. It is an open carriage, with two fine bay horses. Here are the reins, M. de Luynes. Take them and drive your carriage.'

"My husband picked up the imaginary reins, as the ladies tried to stifle their giggles and the men looked on with astonishment. Berini kept giving him instructions.

"'Faster, M. de Luynes, faster. You're late for an appointment. The horses can do it. They're fine, strong animals, and they're still fresh. Urge them on.'

"Gaston did exactly as he was bidden. Finally Berini said, 'You've reached your destination. Now pull the horses up. Whoa, there. Whoa!'

"Then he took the imaginary reins away from him and told him that he would wake up refreshed, in fine health, and remember nothing that had happened. And surely enough, on the third clap poor Gaston did wake up and had no idea he'd made a fool of himself."

Her maid came in with a silver tray bearing a small, exquisitely wrought silver coffeepot and a sugar bowl, cup, and saucer in Sèvres porcelain.

"Would you like me to go on, Chief Inspector?"

"Please do," he urged.

"Berini's next subject was Mme. Compère. He put her to sleep, the same way as before, then led her back to her chair and told her she was taking a bath. Poor Émilie actually went through all the motions of bathing, soaping her arms, and pouring oil over herself. It was amazing, Inspector. That man can make someone do exactly what he wants him to do. But what happened next was even more amazing."

"And what was that?" Blanc asked.

"Émilie—Mme. Compère—was still asleep. Berini told her that, after she woke up, she would stand up and shout 'Hurrah!' every time he mentioned the word 'hat.' He clapped three times; Émilie awoke and, of course, remembered none of the silly things she'd done.

"Then Berini said, 'There is a handsome mahogany table outside. I think, if you looked there, you would find upon it my HAT.'

"And Émilie jumped up and shouted, 'Hurrah!' at the top of her voice. Of course, the rest of us were laughing heartily as poor Émilie looked around in the greatest confusion and embarrassment.

"Berini pretended to be surprised and said, 'Really, Madame. What an extraordinary outburst! I assure you it is a most commonplace HAT.'

"And then poor Émilie jumped to her feet and shouted, 'Hurrah!' again. He repeated the word a third time, and the same thing happened. He put Émilie to sleep once more and told her to forget her previous instructions. I don't remember whether any of us mentioned the word 'hat' again that evening, but if we did nothing happened.

"Berini next chose three gentlemen and put them all under his spell at the same time. He had them take a stroll, shoot at quail, eat ices . . . and then he told them they were outdoors in bitter cold. The room, in fact, was extremely warm, which made their clapping themselves and stamping their feet seem even funnier.

"And that, Inspector Blanc, was Berini's performance."

"Thank you so much, Mme. de Luynes. I want to ask you an indiscreet question, which you needn't answer if you don't want to. How much did you pay Berini?"

Mme. de Luynes laughed. "It is an indiscreet question, but I will answer it. Berini's fee was sixty thousand francs. Now, Chief Inspector, would it be indiscreet of me to ask you why you are making these inquiries?"

Blanc smiled his most charming smile. "At present it would be, Madame. However, if you're still interested, I shall be pleased to do so sometime in the future."

Back out on the street, Blanc thought about Mme. de Luynes's description of Berini's performance. The man was obviously an accomplished and experienced artiste, judging from the way he not merely exhibited a skill but entertained with it; also from the way he built up a performance, exceeding his previous feats with each new subject and working toward a grand climax. But there was one fact out of all the proceedings that stood uppermost in his mind: "Sixty thousand francs for a performance. That's as much as I earn in an entire year."

CHAPTER 8

"My charms must be fading," Daphne observed, "to judge from the way you ran away from here the other night."

"On the contrary, dear lady, you're more beautiful and radiant than ever," Blanc reassured her gallantly. "Your manifold charms enslaved me a long time ago. Now, in addition to everything else, I'm deeply indebted to you. What you said the other night solved my most important case and probably saved my career."

She looked to see if he was joking, and realized he wasn't.

"M. and Mme. de Luynes came to see me backstage after the performance last night. She told me you'd called on her that morning. Why are you so fascinated by this man Berini?"

"Because he is the man who killed those seven people on the Rue Saint-Guillaume," he answered quietly.

Experienced actress though she was, Daphne Perrault did not try to hide her surprise.

"According to the papers that man—the one they call Léon the Frog—is the murderer."

"The papers were told what to print."

"Why?"

"The police needed an official suspect. It was Léon's bad luck to wander into that house and be seen leaving it."

"But how can you be so certain he's not the murderer?" she persisted.

"This," Blanc replied tapping his forehead. "And this." He tapped his heart. "Sometimes the only evidence a policeman has to go on."

"And why are you so certain now that it is Berini?"

Blanc folded his hands, looked down at them, and then looked back up into Daphne's eyes. "I have no proof," he began, "until or unless Berini confesses. There were no witnesses, and all the victims are dead. That, of course, is what the murderer planned. But the evidence against Berini is considerable. Enough, I think, to get a conviction, even without direct proof. Would you like me to elaborate?"

She rested her elbows on her knees, cupped her chin between her fists, and gazed directly at him with her clear blue eyes. "Pray, elaborate."

"First and foremost, Berini has the ability. This crime is unique in the annals of the Paris police. According to Dr. d'Harnoncourt, all seven victims were asleep when their throats were slit. That's something the papers didn't report. There was only one person in Paris at the time who was capable of doing that—putting a roomful of people to sleep—and in so doing he gave himself away.

"Then there is the fact that Berini left Paris on September tenth, the day the murders were committed. According to Dr. d'Harnoncourt again, the victims were killed sometime between eleven and two, probably closer to the latter. According to the porter at the Hotel Baudoins, where Berini was staying, he departed between three and four in the afternoon. What's more, he left in a great hurry, not even bothering to pay his bill properly. He just handed the porter a bag full of money, roughly enough to cover his expenses, and fled."

"Couldn't that be a coincidence?" she asked. "He might have gotten a message that prompted his departure, perhaps one informing him that someone at home was ill."

"Two coincidences," he corrected her. "One, the unique ability to put them to sleep. Two, a hasty departure shortly after the murders were committed."

"I'll admit it's a bit much," she said judiciously.

"But there's more. I grant you that, if that were all, a good lawyer might get him an acquittal. The porter from the hotel further stated that, in his master's absence, Berini's coachman asked him to help him get their trunks downstairs and onto their coach. So obviously Berini had informed him of their departure the night before—or, more likely, that morning.

"I confess the idea of a letter arriving for him hadn't occurred to me. But that's something that can be checked easily with the *patron* and his employees."

"Why did Berini pay his bill at the hotel? If he committed the terrible crime of murdering seven people, would the lesser crime of skipping without paying a hotel bill have mattered?"

"That," said Blanc, with a twinkle in his eye, "is spoken like a true thespian. The actor who steals out of the inn without paying for his room and board."

"I've done it," she said in all seriousness. "When I was young and hungry."

"I know. But Berini wasn't hungry. If he'd skipped without paying, what would the porter have done? Informed his boss immediately, of course, and Roncard would in turn have run to the police. That was the last thing in the world Berini wanted: the police hot on his trail.

"Incidentally, have you any idea what his fee was? Your friend Mme. de Luynes told me. Sixty thousand francs!"

Daphne whistled appreciatively.

"Here in Paris, the city with the greatest number of theaters in all Europe, Berini chose to perform in private salons before limited and carefully selected groups of people. He was *the* great social attraction in Paris, according to Mme. de Luynes, and commanded a quite immodest fee. There were other salons whose hostesses were dying to have him, yet he left here, abruptly and in great haste. Daphne, have you ever heard of an artiste leaving a town while the pickings were still good?"

She shook her head.

"What, then, is the inevitable conclusion?"

"He was running away," she answered obediently.

"Also," he went on, "one can't help wondering why he didn't perform at one of the theaters."

Daphne stared at him with all the intensity of her gaze as Andromaque on the stage. "Why?" she asked, in the voice that thrilled audiences at the Odéon.

"Because, *ma chérie*, the man in the street goes to the theater. But he doesn't get invited to the best salons. Berini's exclusiveness was not a matter of snobbery, but practicality. As it is, it took the police, in the person of your obedient servant, two weeks to even become aware of his existence. But if hundreds, even thousands, of people had seen him perform, someone might have caught on a lot sooner."

"So in fact the police have two suspects, either one of whom could be convicted on the basis of evidence. The first of them was seen leaving the house, and admitted he was there. The second was unseen and unidentified, yet that is the suspect you favor."

Blanc gazed at her admiringly. "Mademoiselle, you have a fine analytical mind, in addition to great beauty."

"The two aren't incompatible. But thank you for the compliment anyway. But it is still only your supposition that Berini was at that house. You said there was other evidence."

"Indeed, yes. If my supposition is correct, and I'm certain it is, Berini had to get back *from that house* to his hotel, and he wasn't about to take a leisurely stroll. You see, from the manner of his departure, what a hurry he was in. Therefore—"

"He took a carriage!" she interrupted.

"Quite so. And we know from which neighborhood and at what time of day he took it. Every coachman in Paris is licensed, and the search has been on since yesterday. By tomorrow I guarantee you the man will be in my office. And with his evidence in court, well. . . . Coincidence number three? How many such coincidences will a jury swallow? Add to these the fact that Berini registered under a false name—well, granted that's going too far. He used his professional name. But he did give a false nationality and address."

"Why?"

"He has a new name and a new identity. In case there was trouble, that would throw the police off his trail. But that wasn't his main reason. If his victims, or potential victims, had known who he was, not only wouldn't they have sat still for him, they would have run for their lives."

"Didn't they recognize him?"

"They'd probably never seen him before. It is possible to wrong someone, terribly, shamefully, without even being aware of that person's existence. Or, for that matter, giving a damn."

"Why did Berini kill those people?"

Blanc leaned back against the couch and drummed with his fingers upon the velvet material. "That is where Berini made his only mistake. He hadn't expected to be discovered, and he doesn't expect to be caught. Yes, his motive. That's the ironic part of the whole thing. If he hadn't killed the three women, the chances are good that, even with a written confession, he might have been acquitted."

The coachman's name was Marcel Jonell, and in mid-morning of the following day, Saturday, September 26, he found himself standing in Chief Inspector Blanc's office. Cartier was the one who'd found him. He stood there awkwardly, looking from one of the inspectors to the other, and playing with his hat, which he held in his hand.

"There's no need to be nervous, M. Jonell," Blanc assured him. "Just tell me again what you already told Inspector Cartier here."

"Well, sir, I picked up this gentleman on Rue Saint-Dominique at about half past two on Thursday, September tenth. I remember that day because it was my youngest daughter's birthday. Agathe, her name is, and she was six that day. My wife asked me to be home early, so that we could have a little celebration. She was baking a cake.

"Well, as I was saying, it was about half past two. I'd just finished eating lunch at the Alsacienne—"

Blanc and Cartier both knew the place, a cafe on the Rue Galande, where coachmen congregated.

"—and I was looking for my first fare of the afternoon. I was headed toward the Boulevard des Invalides, hoping to pick up a swell, when this gentleman hailed me as I drove along the Rue Saint-Dominique."

"In which direction was he walking?" Blanc broke in. "Was he walking toward you, or in the same direction you were headed?"

"In the same way I was going, sir. I remember that because I saw him from the back, and even so I could see he was a swell. Elegant, sir. Real elegant. I've been a coachman for twelve years, and I can always spot a true gentleman, even from the back. Well, he turned around and hailed me. He must have heard the clopping of Dauphin. That's my horse. He hailed me and told me to take him to the Hotel Baudoins.

"He was a real gentleman, sir. I remember he wore a beautiful diamond stickpin in his cravat. Beautiful, it was. He also gave me ten francs. A very generous gentleman he was too."

Cartier had the man's address, and M. Jonell was permitted to rejoin Dauphin, who was no doubt waiting patiently in front of the prefecture.

"It had to be Berini," Blanc said when the two men were alone. He made a mental note to inquire about the stickpin. "As for our search of the city, I think we can call our men off. He's made his dust."

"Unless he's in hiding," Cartier ventured. "But then, he'd need a confederate to bring him food."

"An elegant man, a real gentleman. He wears a diamond in his cravat, carries a gold watch and chain, is fastidious, extremely demanding, and earns sixty thousand francs for a single performance. Tell me, Cartier, can you visualize someone like that hiding out in a wretched attic, or in someone's cellar, and living on cold scraps?"

Cartier grinned and shook his head. "It's strange, Chief. We know so much about this man: his tastes, his habits, his manners, how he dresses, what he likes to eat. Yet none of us has ever laid eyes on him."

"It is unusual," Blanc agreed. "But then, so is the man himself. No, not just unusual, quite extraordinary. He has developed a unique power, one that could have made him a fortune. Instead he used it to destroy the people on whom he'd sworn vengeance years before. That seems to have been the burning goal of his life. Vengeance. Perhaps, for all we know, he studied and developed the science of animal magnetism with that very goal in mind. Everything else, all the performances, the traveling, the reputation were merely a preparation toward that end. I should like to ask him about that."

Cartier was about to tell his chief that he hoped he'd get the chance, but decided against it. "What do you want me to do next, Chief?" he asked.

"Ride around to the various prefectures and tell our inspectors to call their men off. Then go home and pray for a sunny day tomorrow so that we can all enjoy a pleasant Sunday."

After Blanc had dispatched Cartier, he went across the street to the Ministry of Police to see Fouché. The Minister looked up inquiringly as the Chief Inspector entered his office.

"He's left Paris," Blanc said in reply to the unasked question.

"I expected as much," Fouché replied. "The man would have been a fool to stay around here, and we're plainly not dealing with a fool. Still, it was necessary to search. It would have been worse than awkward for the police if we'd looked for him all over Europe, only to find he was hiding here under our very noses. Well, Chief Inspector, what do you propose to do next?"

"I propose to flush him out." Blanc had taken the seat facing the Minister. "We have the advantage, and I mean to use it. Berini thinks he's safe. Thanks to your imaginative efforts, the papers have everyone convinced the police think they've got their man. Surely he must be following the case. Now we must attain new heights of fabrication. The papers must report, in detail, about Léon's trial, and then his execution. It sounds a bit farfetched, I grant you, but it can be done."

Fouché nodded in agreement. "Yes, it can. The journals have printed stories in the past that have had less basis in reality than this one. I think I see what you're getting at."

"I'm certain you do. When Berini left Paris, he probably intended never to come here again. A pity for him, because this city was such a rich source of income, but he simply couldn't risk it. But with another man tried, and condemned, and executed for the murders, the case would be closed. He wouldn't be running much of a risk then, would he?"

"How do you propose to get him back?" Fouché asked.

"I don't know yet. That will depend to a great degree on where he is. But we haven't reached that particular bridge yet. In the meantime, I want to study my man. I want to learn as much as I can about him. I already feel as though I know him, simply because I understand the overbearing passion that has ruled all of his adult life. Now I want to study him in finer detail. I want to find out, from the people at the Hotel Baudoins, how he spent his Sundays, where he went to find amusement, whether he liked women, and what sort of women, what books he liked to read."

"Ah, yes," the Minister smiled. "The famous Blanc method."

"There are those who sneer at it."

"I don't," Fouché said. "Do you think he's gone back to Geneva?"

"I don't think he's gone back to Geneva, because I don't think he came from there. At any rate, he'd be a fool to go there, and as you said, we're not dealing with a fool. Running off to Geneva would be little better than not leaving Paris at all. The city is part of the French Empire. Tell me, M. le Ministre, if you had been planning your revenge for years, and had evolved a carefully crafted plan for attaining that revenge, and a well-prepared escape, where would you go?"

Fouché considered the question for a few moments. "I would go beyond the reach of the French law."

Cartier's prayers must have been answered. Sunday, September 27, was a beautiful, sun-filled day. The birds were actually singing in the elm trees that lined both sides of the street when Blanc's coach stopped in front of Daphne's house, at number 22 Rue Saint-Honoré. The two of them drove off to the Place Saint-Gervais and its famous Gothic church.

They arrived in time for the late mass, the one Blanc had been looking forward to for so long. The one he'd been promising himself for months but that something always seemed to come up to prevent him from hearing. It was at this mass that François Gervais Couperin, the great-nephew of Couperin le Grand, presided at the oldest organ in Paris, as had his family for three generations before him. He played music by two of his illustrious forebears, Louis Couperin and Couperin le Grand.

The music of the great instrument swelled and diminished, filling the vast edifice with great gusts of sound, dwindling down to a thin trickle, and then swelling again into new mighty blasts. It reminded all who would listen of the glory that had once been French music.

Blanc's thoughts couldn't help straying to the past glories of French literature: Corneille, Racine, Molière. Whatever else the Empire might accomplish, it wasn't giving the world any great playwrights or composers. The theaters seemed to present at least one new play each week, either a witless farce that wasn't worth the few hours or francs spent attending it, or a lumbering tragedy that was, quite unintentionally, funnier than the previous week's comedy.

Following mass, Blanc and Daphne went to Rose's for lunch. "You've been awfully quiet," he remarked over their *escalopes de veau.*

"I seem to remember that, the last time we went out together, I made an innocent remark that sent you dashing away like a hound after the foxes."

Blanc laughed. "A quite appropriate description. I thought I'd been forgiven for that."

She smiled. "Of course you have. I just didn't want it to happen again."

"Hardly likely now. It will be some time before we hear of our mystifying friend again."

"And what do you plan to do in the meantime?"

"I mean to devote myself to the worship of music, the joys of love, and the pleasures of food."

She considered this for a moment, and then nodded in approval. "A worthy pastime. You could have put it another way around. The joys of food and the pleasures of love. Have you heard Martini's latest song, 'Plaisir d'Amour'?"

"Yes, I have. I agree with its sentiments, and I like the tune. It's ironic; that man probably can't remember how many operas and masses he's written. Yet if he's remembered at all it will probably be for that one little song. How did you like the music this morning?"

"I did, considering the fact that I don't really like organs. There's something so . . . solemn, so awesome about them. At times, especially with those low, muffled tones, they raise a panic in my breast. Then I feel as though I were staring death in the face."

"I'm sure there are others who feel that way. Yet it is the

greatest of instruments, and what you heard this morning was the glory of French music, along with Lully and Rameau."

"Lully was an Italian by birth," she reminded him.

"And Martini is German. His real name is Schwartzendorf, or something like that. Yet both are Frenchmen by adoption. It's a sad state of affairs when all we have to offer the world today is a Martini or a Lesueur. Your friend Mme. de Luynes is really a quite charming woman, but her taste in music is abominable."

"She told me she thought you were a charming man. She also said something else about you, though."

"Really," he said, looking at her over the rim of his wine glass. "What was that?"

"She said that, despite all the charm, she felt pity toward anyone you ever decided to pursue. You struck her as the sort of man who would never, never give up until you had caught him."

"A most discerning lady," he observed.

After lunch they rode to Longchamp, where they strolled on the path along the Seine where, in 1256, Saint Isabelle had founded her abbey. There was little traffic on the river that day, and men and boys were lazily engaged in fishing along both banks. Blanc was carrying his hat in his hand, as city dwellers were wont to do when strolling in the countryside.

Daphne wore a dress of topaz silk and a toque of the same color. The day was so warm that she had left her cape in Blanc's coach. She was truly a vision to delight and dazzle the eye, wearing a frock and headpiece that matched the color of her golden hair.

"I don't know why," Blanc remarked, "but ever since I was a small boy I always thought of spring as the season of rebirth and reawakening, and autumn as a time of resignation. I suppose I still do."

"Perhaps it's some ancient instinct in us that derives from Proserpine and the rebirth of the earth each spring. I love the ancient myths. Those gods and goddesses are so human."

"Possibly because they were created by man in his image, and with all his failings and weaknesses. Yet autumn, too, has its mellow beauty.

"With song and dance the peasants hail
The happiness of harvest home.
And then from Bacchus' glowing cup
They end their joy in slumber prone."

"What's that?" she asked.

"It's from an Italian sonnet describing autumn. There's more. It goes on to tell how the peasants all fall asleep from the wine, and the next morning a hunt rides by, with horns blowing and hounds pursuing the wearied fox. It must have been your remark over lunch that reminded me of it."

"I spent my childhood in the streets of Paris. You grew up in the farming region of the Auvergne. Is it true, the poem's description of autumn in the countryside, I mean?"

"It wasn't that idyllic. But basically, I suppose yes, it is."

A man near them who had been standing absolutely still holding a rod pulled on his line and brought up a long pike from the Seine.

They rode back into town and stopped off at Frascati for ices. Then, with darkness coming on, they returned to Daphne's house, on the Rue Saint-Honoré. Once inside, in the foyer, she looked at him with a certain air of challenge in her eyes. "Did you mean what you said earlier today about devoting yourself to the joys of love?"

He looked directly into her eyes and answered her lightly taunting tones in all solemnity. "Mademoiselle, I assure you I meant every syllable of it."

On Monday morning Blanc returned to the Hotel Baudoins. He questioned Édouard, the day porter, again. That worthy confirmed the description of the diamond stickpin and stated further that he had never seen Berini without it or without his mahogany walking stick with its ivory handle. From his other remarks, Blanc strengthened the impression he already had, that of a man who liked to live well and knew how to live well.

In answer to his question about women, Édouard seemed to think that Berini had an eye for the ladies. They certainly had an eye for him! Although, the porter hastily added, in the sev-

eral weeks he'd lived at the hotel he'd never seen him take a
woman up to his room.

"How did he treat you and the other employees here?"
Blanc asked.

The other knew exactly what he meant. "It's not just that he
tipped well, Inspector Blanc, although he did that. He treated
us like human beings. Always a good morning and a good afternoon. He asked me one time if I was married, and I told
him I had a wife and four children. After that, he always asked
me how they were. He was—"

"I know," Blanc said. "A gentleman. A true gentleman."

Blanc called on another hostess at whose salon Berini had
entertained. Mme. Montaigu, who resided on the Rue Desèze,
was not nearly as cooperative as Mme. de Luynes. But then,
Blanc didn't have Daphne as an introduction to her. Like
many others of her social circle, Mme. Montaigu considered
policemen as servants and social inferiors. (He could imagine
the sort of remarks Édouard would have made about her as a
hotel guest.)

"I don't understand the reason for this inquiry, Inspector.
M. Berini didn't steal anything from my house."

"I never implied that he did, Madame. I merely wish to ask
a few questions about him."

"As I have not made any complaints, I fail to see any reason
for this visit."

Blanc tried to restrain himself—admittedly a difficult task.

"Mme. Montaigu, I am asking you, as a citizen of France, to
cooperate with the Paris police in answering a few simple
questions. I promise to take as little of your valuable time as
possible."

The appeal to her patriotism seemed to mollify the great
lady somewhat. Still grudgingly, she consented to answer the
Chief Inspector's questions. She had had twenty guests the
night Berini had entertained. Yes, the man had been exasper-
ating, but he was, after all, *the* great attraction in Paris society.

Evidently Berini gave the same demonstration in every
salon. Blanc's respect for his opponent was growing by leaps
and bounds. The man despised Mme. Montaigu and her kind.
He was as arrogant and demanding with them as he dared be,

and he squeezed as much money out of these people as he possibly could. . . .

"Is there anything else you wish to know, Inspector?"

"I think that will do for the present, Mme. Montaigu. I thank you for your kind cooperation."

He was back again at his regular table at his favorite cafe. Who was it who said that yesterday's novelty becomes tomorrow's commonplace? It was all too true. He'd had two small out-of-town engagements, and in each case it was a devil of a long way to travel for one performance. True, he was not the inventor of animal magnetism, nor its first practitioner, but unlike Professor Mesmer, he was not a physician. He used the power strictly to entertain, and with no pretense of scientific research. In that respect he was, indeed, unique; probably the only artiste of his kind in the world. Some said that Cagliostro had possessed the power (he unconsciously fingered his diamond stickpin), but he rather doubted it.

He was playing with the idea of touring Italy. That, of course, would involve a great deal of travel, but their larger towns were good for at least two or three nights. Then, perhaps, Switzerland again. That fool Prinklhof was working on it, but like all of his breed—theatrical managers and theater owners—his promises always exceeded his performance.

Josef came over to him with the afternoon papers. He looked through them eagerly for stories about the Rue Saint-Guillaume murders. And, sure enough, there they were. It looked as if the Paris police had gotten their hooks into some poor fool, a thief called Léon the Frog. If the stories were to be believed (he knew journalists as a far from honest lot), this Léon had actually been into the house that afternoon and, worse, had been seen leaving it. There seemed little chance of the poor devil's escaping the guillotine.

He was strongly tempted to write a letter to the Paris police, assuring them, in enough detail to make himself believable, that M. Léon was innocent. He was on the verge of asking Josef for paper, pen, and ink, when at the last second he restrained himself. His plan had been to get clean away, without a trace, and he had succeeded perfectly. His plan had not included writing the police taunting letters, or helping them to the solution of a case that was, after all, their problem.

He returned his attention to the papers. They all carried basically the same story and the same details. If one wanted to be cynical about it, the conviction of another man was all to his advantage, though totally unplanned. It meant there would not be an unsolved case to haunt him the rest of his life. Yes, perhaps he would go to Italy. . . .

Despite the use of messengers on horseback and semaphores, it took two weeks before word came back to the Ministry of Police. On Tuesday, October 13, Blanc received a message asking him to call on the Minister.

"You were right again, Blanc," was Fouché's greeting to him as he entered the Minister's office. "I've just gotten a report from my spies. He is in Vienna."

Blanc experienced no feeling of exultation at having deduced his opponent's moves correctly. "A country, Austria, with which we are currently at peace, but with which we have no treaty of extradition," Blanc observed.

Fouché nodded. "So he's escaped us."

"Not necessarily," Blanc said.

CHAPTER 9

"He lives at 237 The Graben," Fouché said, "strolls along St. Michael Square, and visits the Cafe Hammel each afternoon. Tell me, Blanc, what made you so sure it was Vienna?"

"I wasn't sure, but all sorts of bits and pieces pointed to it. He probably left France when he was a very young man. He studied under Mesmer—where else but in Vienna? This is only conjecture, but Vienna is a beautiful, sophisticated city. It is also the capital of the country most strongly opposed to France on the Continent. The place, in other words, where he would feel safest. Therefore, why not establish residence there?"

"Of course, it has been twice occupied by French troops," Fouché commented, "but that hardly matters. There he probably passes for an Austrian. Do you mean to tell me that Vienna was just a lucky guess on your part?"

"Let's call it a calculated one. Berini gave his coachman's name as Charles Steiner on his registry here. But the porter at the Baudoins twice referred to him as Karl. He must have heard Berini call him that. Karl Steiner is an Austrian name."

Fouché chuckled. "It's the little things in life that trip us up. You said he's not necessarily beyond our reach. I hope you weren't going to suggest kidnapping him."

Blanc shook his head. "Hardly. The last thing the French Empire needs is another duc d'Enghien affair."

"I agree. Besides, it's impractical: The distance between Vienna and Paris is too great to carry a man by force. Also, neither Talleyrand nor the Emperor would ever approve. It would jeopardize the delicate peace agreement between France and Austria. What, then, do you suggest?"

"That we lure him back."

Fouché raised his eyebrows. "Has he a mistress here in Paris? I wasn't aware of it."

"I don't think so. In any case, a woman wouldn't be enough of a lure to bring him back here. I've been studying my man carefully these past two weeks. Berini—whatever his real name is—is a complex creature, a man of many parts. But I think I've found his weakness."

"And that is—"

"His vanity. The man is inordinately vain. Perhaps we can play on that."

Fouché listened attentively.

"We have a place here in Paris," Blanc went on, "an institution, almost, that is the most renowned of its kind in the world. Performing there is considered an honor, quite aside from the remunerative fees. It is the dream of every act in Europe to perform there, but only the very best are chosen."

"The Cirque," Fouché said.

"Exactly. Do you know the director, M. Lenoir?"

"Yes, I do. We'd have to take him into our confidence, but I believe Antoine Lenoir is a man who can respect a confidence. By the way, does your friend Léon the Frog have any idea that he's a corpse?"

It was Blanc's turn to chuckle. "Leon isn't getting any papers in his cell. And in any case, they wouldn't do him much good. He can't read. But I haven't read about his execution today."

"The story will appear in tomorrow's papers. And, of course, I'll make sure they get into the Austrian papers. The English, Dutch, and Austrian papers have been following the case avidly anyway. They take their stories directly out of the Paris papers."

There was a moment's silence as the two men regarded each other.

"There's no guarantee he'll take the bait," Blanc said.

"Of course not. But shall we pay a call on M. Lenoir?"

Blanc had met M. Lenoir before, and Fouché seemed to be on good terms with him. The circus director was a short, stout, well-dressed man of about fifty, who wore a handsome wig to hide his complete baldness. He was fascinated by the story his two visitors told him.

"The ironic part of it is," Lenoir said, "that I did want him to perform at the Cirque. I was going to write him a letter, if I could ever track him down. I wanted to talk to him when he was here, a few weeks ago, but he left town before I got the chance. Now it appears as though he never will perform for us."

"No, he won't," Fouché said. "Whatever may happen, that much is certain."

"A pity," Lenoir remarked. "He really is an extraordinary performer. I saw him when he was in Paris three years ago. You wouldn't let him do just one performance for us and then grab him?"

Fouché shook his head. "I'm afraid it's out of the question, Lenoir. Even if you are serious about that, which I doubt. We want to use the Cirque as bait to lure him back to France. Would you write Berini a letter, if Blanc and I dictated it?"

"Of course, gentlemen. I am entirely at your disposal." He took pen and paper and waited for the two police officials to begin.

"My Dear M. Berini," Blanc said, "I had the great pleasure of seeing you perform when you appeared here in our beautiful city of Paris three years ago. Yours is truly one of the most extraordinary acts I have ever witnessed in my . . ."

"Twenty."

". . . twenty years as a theatrical director. In fact, I can say without hesitation that your performance is unique. I have literally never seen anything to compare with it, either here at home or in my voluminous travels."

Fouché nodded his approval, and Lenoir was beaming.

"Please don't hesitate to interrupt me, M. Lenoir, if you think there's anything out of character. Anything that might arouse the slightest suspicion."

"On the contrary, Chief Inspector, you have the style down perfectly. Artistes are notoriously susceptible to flattery, and theatrical managers are equally notorious for their self-esteem."

"I had hoped to discuss with you, during your recent visit to

our beloved city, the possibility of an engagement at the renowned and venerable institution of which I have the honor to
be General Director. Unfortunately, pressing matters of a personal nature prevented me from coming to see you, and by the
time I was able to do so you had departed. An acquaintance of
mine, an Austrian, Herr Schindler, told me you lived in Vienna
(where you are regarded as a great celebrity), and gave me
your address."

Blanc and Fouché looked at each other as though to say, If
only he swallows that, all the rest will be easy going.

"What I propose, dear M. Berini, is that you perform at the
Cirque, commencing November 16, for an engagement of two
weeks, which engagement is to be extended for an indefinite
period should the attendance and enthusiasm of our Parisian
audiences warrant it (which I do not for a moment doubt).

"The fee, for one performance each evening, excepting Sundays, would be . . ." He looked at M. Lenoir. "One hundred
eighty thousand francs?"

Lenoir nodded.

". . . one hundred eighty thousand francs per week. This is
the highest fee, M. Berini, that any artiste has ever received in
the entire history of the Cirque. Even the Follenzas and Munio
did not receive this much. Of course, it is understood that your
name will head the list of artistes in all printed an-
nouncements.

"It is my sincere hope, dear sir, that the Cirque will have the
honor of presenting you to a large Parisian public, who are (I
am certain you are aware) sympathetic in their regard and
generous with their applause for true artistes.

"I look forward eagerly to your earliest reply, and am

"Your admirer and obedient servant—"

Lenoir, whose pen had been racing along, looked up at
Blanc, his face creased in a beatific smile. "It's a masterpiece,
Inspector Blanc. I couldn't have done better myself. I'll copy it
over and send the letter off with today's post."

As Blanc and Fouché were strolling along the Rue Saint-An-
toine, the Minister said, "I was wondering how you were going
to get around that business of the address. Do you think that
will arouse his suspicions?"

Blanc shrugged. "We can hope the prestige of the engagement and the generous fee will dull his warning senses. It's a famous street in Vienna, The Graben. Beethoven lives there, and Mozart did for a time. The whole city probably *does* know where Berini lives."

Fouché nodded. "Who is Herr Schindler?"

"I haven't the faintest idea."

First the Parisians and then the rest of France, followed by Holland, Austria, and England, read about the trial and execution of the man called Léon the Frog. They read about his full confession, his repentance, and his beheading with that special fascination the public always feels toward sensational murder cases. This one had an ending that satisfied everyone (except presumably the murderer). The Paris police had scored another success, justice was once more triumphant, and the criminal was properly repentant before meeting his well-deserved end.

At five o'clock on a cold, overcast morning, October 19, the condemned man was led out into the courtyard of Meudon. His hands were tied behind his back, his shirt was open at the neck, and he shivered noticeably in the early-morning chill. A slight drizzle was beginning to fall. A few onlookers crossed themselves, like the good Christians they were. The condemned man climbed up to the platform, knelt, and placed his head on the guillotine, over the basket. He was assisted in this by the executioner, who then took his place behind the instrument. There was a brief moment of absolute silence, punctuated only by the sound of rain falling on the rooftops, and then with a whoosh the blade fell, swiftly and accurately.

Paul Marais was one reader who wasn't satisfied. His first reaction, as leading journalist of the *Journal de Paris*, was one of disgruntlement because he hadn't been permitted to cover the trial. Then he began to wonder exactly who did cover it. Who did attend the sessions, and who described the execution. That last description was correct in every detail, but it could as easily have applied to a hundred other executions.

He began by asking questions among his fellow scribes. Platant, Delcomb, Tours . . . each of them claimed ignorance of the aforementioned events. That was strange, Marais thought, when one considered that this was the most sensational murder trial Paris had experienced in years.

He went around to the Palais de Justice and began asking questions of the clerks, all of whom he knew. They professed ignorance of the whole thing. Then he questioned a few lawyers, and finally a judge or two. No, the *magistrat* assured him, he personally had not presided at the trial. Surely, others of his colleagues must have done so.

Marais was a slender man, whose thinness made him appear taller than he was. He had a narrow, pock-marked face, small, beady eyes, a hawklike nose, and an altogether sharp, crafty look about him. He dressed carelessly; one suspected his linen was not always clean. After more than a dozen years as a journalist, there was scarcely anyone in Paris he didn't know. He was known to possess cunning, and people in places of authority had reason to fear him. He had something else as well: an instinct for self-preservation. Despite the sharpness of his pen, he had survived the Republic, the Directory, and the Consulate.

"Marais, my lad," he said to himself, tapping his beak of a nose, "*this* has never led you astray yet. And it tells you that there is more behind this affair than anyone is letting on."

Why all the secrecy? he wondered. The Code Napoléon expressly forbade a trial without observers—and he hadn't found one yet! Two of the four victims were really important, the diplomat and the lawyer. Was this, perhaps, more than a simple case of murder?

The direct approach, of course, would be to talk to the man who had been in charge of the case, Inspector Blanc. He didn't get along well with Blanc, though, and he had no illusions about the other man's opinion of him. True, the man was said to be incorruptible (he himself wasn't), but he hardly considered that a virtue or a recommendation for high position.

There was a place where one could get more information than anywhere else in Paris, and he knew it well. He went to the Ninth Arrondissement and visited several of the wineshops. Au Vache Rouge, Le Ver dans la Fromage, Le Grenadier, La Lanterne Jaune—he went to all of them and asked the same question.

"Where's Marie?"

"She hasn't been in here today," the *patron* said. He was in the Lanterne Jaune. "But I wouldn't be surprised if she was tipsy by now. She hasn't been the same since her boyfriend lost his head." The *patron* laughed, as if this were a good joke.

"Any idea where I can find her?" Marais asked. He himself had had a glass at each of his ports of call.

The *patron* shrugged as if to say, Who knows? With women like Marie, who can ever tell?

"She'll grump for a while, then she'll take up with someone else. You'll see. They always do."

It was late afternoon by now, and dusk was already beginning to settle over the narrow, winding streets. Marais liked this section of Paris. Some said it was dangerous after dark, but he had never found it so. He'd always felt there was more danger at St.-Cloud, at Versailles, and at the Palais du Luxembourg.

He finally caught up with Marie in a small wineshop on the Rue Cloche called simply Louis. The establishment, a dark, tiny room with four tables, was named not after one of the kings of France but the shop's owner.

Marie was, as the expression goes, in her cups. A swarthy woman of indeterminate age, with straggly brown hair that fell over washed-out blue eyes, she managed to look both undernourished and blowsy. It took the merest mention of Léon the Frog to set her off.

"Those bastards!" she said. "Those lousy, rotten bastards! They killed him. They killed Léon."

"The papers say he confessed," Marais prompted her.

"Then, they must have tortured him, those *coignes*. They'll do anything to get a confession. Everyone knows that."

"Did Léon kill those people?"

"Léon?" She tried to laugh, but it quickly turned into a sob. "Léon couldn't kill a flea. He was afraid of his own shadow. I'm always amazed he became a burglar. I hear he was good at it too, although he got caught a couple of times. I kept begging him to quit, that he was getting too old for the game. He al-

ways said just one more time, then we'd buy a small wineshop
and live off that. And now they've gone and killed him."

The tears rolled down her unwashed face. Marais motioned
for Louis to fill their glasses again.

"You know who was in charge of the case. Inspector Blanc,"
he said.

"I know. They told me. That son-of-a-bitch got hold of Léon
and then wouldn't let him go. He got a confession out of him,
and then they killed him."

Marais commiserated with the woman for a few more minutes. He kept his growing suspicions to himself, as to whether
there had, in fact, been a trial or execution at all. Suspicions
were one thing, but he wanted some proof.

He went on home to his room on the Rue Juvier and thought
about the matter some more. He was not the sort of man to
fight with his pen for the freedom of an unjustly imprisoned
man or to campaign for the rehabilitation of someone's good
name.

No, far from it. There was a story here. A really important
story, and he wanted it. Despite all the reports in the papers
there was no evidence whatever that a trial and execution had
taken place. On the contrary, there were enough questions to
raise serious doubts about the truth of these reports.

He remembered what Marie had said about Léon. "He
couldn't kill a flea." It would be out of keeping for Blanc to
bring charges against such a man, although he himself knew
full well to what lengths men would go to save their careers.

But, as he was almost certain there had been no trial or execution, there had to be another reason behind it all. What,
then? Obviously, the police wanted people to believe the case
was closed. Why? To protect their own skins? But the case
wasn't that old, and Blanc wasn't a man who gave up that
easily.

Correction, Marais. The police wanted one man in particular
to think they were satisfied. The real murderer, of course.
Again that magical question: Why? To bring him out of hiding? A strong possibility. But why go to so much trouble—to
plant those stories—unless they knew who it was.

Congratulations, Marais. I think you've hit on it. The police know who the murderer is, but they can't get their hands on him. Because he's in hiding? A possibility, a strong possibility. Then, when he reads about the case being closed, he climbs out of his hiding place, strolls down the Champs Élysées, and the police tap him on the shoulder and say, "M. X, we arrest you for the murder of seven people."

Let us now consider the alternate possibility. The police not only know who the murderer is, they know where he is. And still they can't get their hands on him. Why? There can be only one answer to that. They can't touch him because he's beyond the reach of French law. In other words, he's outside the French Empire. And this campaign in the papers is a desperate ruse by Blanc to lure the murderer back.

Are you spinning yarns, Marais? Is it all too farfetched? If you could get proof that Léon was alive, that would make your premise almost a certainty, wouldn't it?

The following morning, Marais went to the prison on the Rue Meudon and tried to talk to the governor. That official, he was informed, was too busy to see him. Marais shrugged it off. He hadn't expected to be told the truth, but he fancied he was able to tell, by now, when he was being lied to. The question that had been plaguing him since last night was, Where were they keeping Léon? At the prefecture? In Blanc's own house? Hidden away somewhere in the country? The last was a distinct possibility, until one realized that Léon was a child of Paris who had probably never seen the countryside in his life. They would need an armed guard over him night and day to keep him from running off. In fact, if one needed to keep a man hidden, a man who was officially dead, what better place than in prison? An old prison, with underground cells.

Marais, you have it! La Pitié. He was pleased with himself at having outfoxed Blanc. And he was certain he was right, but he needed proof. He knew the governor of the Pitié, Sorrel. On his way over to the ancient prison-hospital, he thought about concocting a story that would explain his visit there. Duchamp, that was it. Duchamp, the knife murderer, had been wounded and was being held there.

Much to his surprise, he was granted an interview with

Duchamp, under the surveillance of two armed guards. It was an interview he hadn't really wanted, but, good journalist that he was, he made the most of it. Afterward he spoke to Sorrel as the two of them were walking through the corridors.

"Tell me, M. le Gouverneur, who is being held in the old underground cells right now?"

"Why, no one, Marais," the old city official replied. "You know those cells haven't been used in years."

Marais knew for a fact that they had. "I wonder if I might see them," he persisted. "They might make an interesting story for the *Journal*'s readers. The contrast between the Old Regime with its barbaric treatment of the condemned, and the Empire's humane, enlightened attitude toward prisoners."

"That's out of the question," Sorrel said. "No one is permitted down there."

"But surely an empty cell—"

"The area has been walled off," Sorrel said, with finality.

It wasn't proof, Marais thought, but then, he'd hardly expected to be brought face to face with Léon. Why would the governor consent to let him interview a notorious criminal, and then refuse to show him a few empty cells? Because *someone* was being held down there. Someone, he felt certain, about whom Sorrel had been given strict orders. He racked his brains in an effort to think about any other citizen of Paris who had disappeared from sight, and could think of no one.

Marais was frankly pleased with his own cleverness, and perhaps justifiably so. But he had made one grave mistake, not in his deductions, but in another area entirely. He had been so taken with his own cleverness that he'd underestimated his adversary. Like Blanc's colleague Chief Inspector Clement of the Gaming and Racing Department, Governor General Sorrel presented to the world a stolid, blunt appearance that hid a shrewd and quick mind.

No sooner had Marais departed than Sorrel sat down at his writing desk and jotted down a note to the Minister of Police, voicing his suspicions at the journalist's visit. He might, he added, be entirely mistaken, but he felt certain that M. Fouché would want to know about the incident. He folded the note, placed on it his official seal, and ordered one of his guards to take it to the Minister immediately.

Marais had supper at a local cafe where he was well known. He then went to the Colombe, a leading hangout for writers and journalists on the Rue de la Ferme. Platant and Tours were already there, and Delcomb joined them shortly after his arrival. They talked about the latest decree, the novel Tours was writing (and had been ever since Marais first knew him and which he would never finish), and between the four of them, polished off six bottles of Pomerol.

When Marais walked back to his quarters alone at half past one, he was certainly not drunk. Neither was he quite sober. He had also consumed a bottle of wine with his supper earlier that evening. As he made his way through the dark streets, he thought contemptuously about his companions. They were men of small talent and limited imagination, and they would never be anything more than they were: second-rate scribes.

Whereas he—what might he not yet accomplish? He was only in his mid-thirties (although he knew he looked older). Just today he had written a better story about Duchamp, without half trying, than anyone else in Paris could manage. He would willingly have written any fiction about Léon—even accusing him of the assassination of Marat—had he been paid to do so. But he had been entirely ignored in this little farce, and that did not suit Paul Marais.

When he got up to his room, he threw himself down on the bed in his clothes. What ought he to do next in his pursuit of his story? Too tired. He would think about it in the morning. . . .

Through a deep, dreamless sleep he heard a steady pounding. At first he thought he'd dreamt it; then he thought it was a neighbor beating against a wall. Finally he realized someone was knocking on the door of his room. He looked at his watch: it was three o'clock.

"Who is it?" he called out.

"Open in the name of the Emperor."

He got up, moved unsteadily to the door, and opened the

latch. There stood two men wearing black hats that hid their faces and black capes that matched the darkness of the night.

"Paul Marais?" one of them asked.

"Yes."

"Come with us."

CHAPTER 10

Whatever else Paul Marais might be, he was not a hypocrite. He never claimed to be a brave man, nor did he now pretend he wasn't frightened. The two men bundled him into a wagon, and off they rolled into the blackness of the night. Seated all alone on a wooden bench in the enclosed back section, in total darkness and with no idea where they were taking him, the leading writer of the *Journal de Paris* freely admitted to himself that he was shaking with terror.

Then, gradually, he got his mind working again. His initial fear, that he was going to be killed, he now dismissed as groundless. He had not the slightest doubt that his abduction had to do with this Léon the Frog business. If the police wanted him dead, they'd had ample opportunity earlier that night to take care of him. A swift crack on the skull while he was walking home through the deserted streets would have done it. His corpse would have been discovered by someone going to work early the next morning, and all Paris would soon have rung with the news that poor Marais had been killed and robbed while staggering home from one of his habitual drinking bouts.

His second idea, while not quite as morbid, was almost equally depressing. He entertained a vision of himself being thrown into one of those underground cells he'd been so eager to see just a few hours earlier. There he could scream to his heart's content about the Code Napoléon, with no one to hear him other than the deaf, senile jailer who brought him a bowl of thin potato soup and a piece of moldy bread twice a day, who neither knew nor cared who he was or why he was there, and who had long since stopped differentiating between the present occupant of this cell and his unfortunate predecessor.

The fact that the second of these was a real possibility somehow failed to cheer him up. Of one thing he was certain: Whatever they had in store for him, he wasn't going to be charged with anything formally. He had broken no law and committed no crime. Therefore, whatever they were going to do would be done clandestinely, as witnessed by the fact that they had come for him in the middle of the night. In other words, he would have no chance to defend himself. This knowledge, too, failed to put him in a properly cheerful frame of mind.

He thought about the infamous affair of the duc d'Enghien in 1804. The secret police had uncovered a Royalist plot against the Consulate. There was some slight evidence against the young Duke, who was at that time residing in Ettenheim, in Baden, across the Rhine. A French force crossed over and, illegally and in violation of neutral territory, kidnapped him and brought him back to France. Following a hasty court-martial, he was condemned to death and executed by firing squad in the Château de Vincennes, still protesting his innocence. All of this, trial and execution, in ninety minutes.

Whether or not Bonaparte himself was involved in the affair, he'd never lived it down. Afterward, Fouché made the classic remark that the French Government's action was worse than a crime: It was stupid.

Marais sincerely hoped—and his interest was more than aesthetic—that the police were not about to commit another stupidity.

The wagon came to a halt. For all his reassurances to himself that nothing violent would happen to him, he felt his heart stop beating. The two men unlocked the door and brought him out roughly. Marais found himself standing in front of the Ministry of Police, and nearly swooned with relief. He was led indoors and down the corridor in the direction of what he knew was Fouché's office. One of the men knocked on the door, a deep voice said, "Enter!" and they brought him in.

In the candlelight he could see Fouché seated behind his desk and Blanc sitting in a chair on one side of the office. The two policemen saluted smartly, left their prisoner standing in the center as the room's chief attraction, and turned and walked out, shutting the door behind them.

"So, M. Marais, we have been going around making inquiries about Léon the Frog, have we?" the Minister said.

Marais knew better than to deny anything Fouché was going to say. He nodded his head dumbly.

"But we know for a fact that Léon is dead, isn't that so? Our leading papers have reported as much, and you of all our citizens, as Paris's foremost journalist, know our papers never lie. Isn't that correct, M. Marais?"

"Yes . . . yes, M. le Ministre," Marais mumbled.

"And digging up dead matter, raising doubts about the validity of the government's word, is both harmful and malicious, isn't it, Monsieur?"

"Yes, sir."

"Oh, sit down, Marais," Fouché said. "You make me ill. I wouldn't mind your making a nuisance of yourself, but you don't even have the courage of your convictions."

Marais wobbled over to the nearest chair and collapsed into it.

"You question the whole business about Léon the Frog, don't you? You don't believe there ever was a trial, you don't think he's dead, and what's more you think the government is calling the case closed to trap the real murderer."

Here was one man whom Marais would never underestimate. He merely nodded his head again.

"Well, suppose I told you your suspicions were correct in every respect."

Marais's head jerked involuntarily upright.

"Suppose I also told you that if you breathe one word of this to anyone, I promise you you'll never see the outside of a prison cell again."

"I . . . I give you my word, M. le Ministre—"

Fouché cut him off. "I have told you the absolute truth about where we stand right now in this case. I am also telling you the truth about what will happen to you if you mention one word about this to another living soul. The charges against you, serious ones, will be obstructing justice, hindering the police in the performance of their duties, and giving aid to a murderer.

"However, as a loyal subject of the Emperor and a patriotic citizen of Paris, I know we can count on your fine cooperation. Isn't that correct, M. Marais?"

"Yes, M. le Ministre," Marais said, much louder and almost joyfully.

"Neither the Chief Inspector nor I ever doubted it for a moment," Fouché remarked dryly. "In return for your splendid cooperation, I promise that you will be the first journalist to learn all the details of the case, directly from Inspector Blanc. And you know that Inspector Blanc and I always keep our word, in all things.

"And now I think it's high time you got back home and resumed your sleep. You'll be needing it, after consuming a bottle of Alsatian Riesling with your *tripes Caen* at dinner, and the better part of two bottles of Pomerol afterward at the Colombe. The two policemen outside will take you back to your house. After all, we wouldn't want anything to happen to you in the dark streets. Good night, M. Marais."

Thinking about the affair in his office the next morning, Blanc couldn't help smiling to himself. An unscupulous scoundrel, that Marais, but what a nose for a story the man had! Of course, he'd figured the whole thing out. (Blanc wondered uneasily how many other people had.) No doubt Marais thought of himself as a practical man and one very much of his time and place. There was no room in his makeup for idealism or spirituality, yet it was that very lack that prevented him from being a truly first-rate writer. He had the skill and sharpness of a Voltaire, but not his sense of justice and morality. He would never be anything more than clever.

Fouché had handled him perfectly last night. Blanc had seen frightened men before, but this one really deserved a prize for sheer abject, debasing, groveling terror. What did he think was going to happen to him? The worst that could have befallen him was exile from Paris, and that would have required an edict from the Emperor.

He got up, went over to the window, and watched the boats

plying their traffic up and down the Seine. There were ominous dark clouds in the sky, like great black feathers; it was
going to rain. Was morality so necessary for a writer? he wondered. France's greatest poet, François Villon, had been a
scoundrel and rogue. But perhaps he only stole when he was
hungry. Perhaps there were two François Villons, the knave
who associated with cutthroats, thieves, and beggars, and the
prodigally gifted poet who gave the French language some of
its most unforgettable lines and phrases.

Perhaps the first one had to consort with the dregs of humanity because no one else would bother with him. The
Church and the nobility praised his verses, when they noticed
him at all, but they didn't give him any money. Being a writer
in those days was not a self-supporting occupation. (Was it
any more so now?) And the second, the other Villon, the great
versifier, gave France so much more than she ever gave him in
return. Prison, exile, hunger, the shadow of the gibbet, the
daily assurance that an empty purse, like an empty stomach,
made a human being mere scum, was all the reward his genius
ever brought him.

He should have been borne through the streets of Paris in
triumph, granted a title, given a life pension and a fine house
to live in!

And of course the two were one and the same man, or he
would not have been François Villon. For when he wrote,
sometimes, in thieves' argot, the language of the streets, he
brought French poetry out of its anachronous medieval armor
and into modern-day dress.

Who would I rather have been, had I lived three and a half
centuries ago, François Villon or the Paris Chief of Police?
(They still had his police records right here at the prefecture.)
There was no question about it in his mind—hunger, gallows,
and all. Who knows? perhaps Marais will be remembered after
all, long after I'm forgotten. He found that the thought didn't
bother him for one second. We each have our own parts to
play on this great stage. His own was to be a police inspector
and do the best job he possibly could. He was quite content
with that role. In fact, he would be perfectly content right now

if the elaborate net he was casting succeeded in ensnaring Berini.

Blanc's greatest concern was that Berini would see through his ruse, as Marais had done (and with the greatest of ease). And yet, he rather thought not. He didn't for a moment doubt the man's brilliance, but although he might be a Frenchman by birth, by this time he really was a foreigner. And he had never been a Parisian. He lacked that intimacy with Paris, its bourgeoisie, its police, its journalists, and its thieves that Marais possessed.

The association that came most readily to mind at the thought of Berini's name was that of Cagliostro. No doubt he had tried to make himself into a Cagliostro sort of personality, a man of great mystery and uncertain origins, possessing almost supernatural powers. And yet there was a great difference between the two. Cagliostro had been a charlatan. (The prefecture also had his police records, the notorious Queen's Necklace affair, and Blanc had studied the case thoroughly.) Berini, on the other hand, was a professional performer who delivered what he promised. In fact, in his last performance in this city, he'd delivered considerably more than he'd promised!

There! Those clouds had burst, and a heavy rain was starting to fall. He watched it travel across the Seine, like a great dark sheet, until it reached the Île du Palais and beat its tattoo against his window panes.

If only, he thought, other events could be predicted that readily.

Another man stood watching the steady downpour through his office window. Georges Desmans, of the law firm of Desmans et fils (he hadn't yet decided whether to retain that name or not), found his thoughts drawn back to that shattering event and its aftermath.

He thought about the letter he'd burned, and whether it would have made any difference in the resolution of the case. It was a moot point now; he could hardly have gone to the police and admitted he'd destroyed a piece of evidence. Also, as it turned out, the solution to the murders had nothing to do with the backgrounds of the four men. A common criminal had slaughtered all his victims.

Or had he? That man, Inspector Blanc, hadn't struck him as a fool. Perhaps that was what the police preferred to believe. He shrugged his shoulders. Who knows, had he taken the letter to them, he would have been politely received, and politely thanked for his assistance? And then they might have placed the letter in some obscure file where they knew it wouldn't be discovered for at least two generations.

Let sleeping dogs lie. He'd heard his father use the expression on several occasions, long before he knew it referred to himself and his friend Pardon. He also knew now, as he'd suspected for some time, that he had been named after Georges Pardon.

He hadn't liked the idea of lying to his sister about his disposition of the letter, but he knew it was for the best. Her head was still filled with old-fashioned, romantic notions, derived from Goethe, about truth, beauty, and honor.

Those qualities had been swept out with the Old Regime, replaced by Liberty, Equality, Fraternity. Ironically enough, his father had been one of those who'd done the sweeping. He didn't blame him. Heavens, no. He'd done the proper thing to ally himself with the winning side. And when that phase was *passé*, he'd had enough sense not to join the Jacobins. (Those fools want to keep the Revolution going forever, his father had once said.)

So now we are in the new age, and Liberty, Equality, Fraternity have been replaced by Greed, Avarice, and Opportunism. Instead of zealots we now have cynics. On the whole an improvement: They do less harm.

What was it about rain, he wondered, that set men's minds wandering? The social season was getting under way in earnest, and he felt that he and his sister had had a respectable period of mourning. It was time to take Michelle out and introduce her to the right people. There were plenty of army officers about, but he would prefer a lawyer or diplomat as an eligible suitor for her.

Lawyer. Diplomat. His mind returned again to the event that had so upset their lives five weeks before. It had been beautifully sunny that morning when his sister had run through the halls of the Palais de Justice and burst into his chambers, hysterical with grief. Unlike himself, she would never comprehend the real meaning behind the event. She was the lucky one. As for himself—

"Let sleeping dogs lie," he said aloud.

Despite the heavy rain, a large audience came out to the Odéon that night to see Racine's *Athalie*. Daphne, as the wicked yet strangely admirable heroine, was magnificent. She seemed taller on the stage than in private life, especially when she played tragedy, and her normally soft voice rang out to the last row of the gallery with a tension and vibrancy that thrilled the audience. More than that, it stirred them.

Seated in his regular box, Blanc felt himself stirred, even though he had seen her play the role several times before. Her head held high, her body erect like a true queen, her gestures sparing yet effective, she gave meaning and urgency to her final speech.

> Que dis-je souhaiter, je me flatte, j'espère
> Qu'indocile à ton joug, fatigué de ta loi,
> Fidèle au sang d'Achab qu'il a reçu de moi,
> Conforme à son aïeul, à son père semblable,
> On verra de David l'héritier détestable,
> Abolir tes honneurs, profaner tes autels,
> Et venger Athalie, Achab et Jézabel.

The audience burst into a storm of applause, yet the actors didn't lose their concentration. They held onto their characters until they were able to complete the scene.

Afterward, as they rode back to Daphne's house in Blanc's carriage, they talked about the play and the night's performance.

"You take drama very seriously, don't you?" she asked him.

"As seriously as you do. When it's well played—and it was well played tonight—I get completely caught up in it. I forget who I am and where I am. I suppose that's why one goes to the theater, isn't it?"

They were back in Daphne's drawing room, and Clarisse had brought in a tray of mushrooms stuffed with snails and a bottle of Haut Médoc.

"Would you have wanted to be an actor—if you hadn't become a policeman, I mean?"

"I never thought I had the voice or stature for an actor. Of course, that is part of being an artist, to transcend one's limitations. It's funny you should ask me that, though. Just this morning I was thinking about what I might have been, had I not become a policeman."

"What is that?"

"A thief, and a poet." He described his thoughts about François Villon, and what had prompted them.

"Then, Marais knows everything now," she said.

"Not everything. He doesn't know whom we're after. He might yet figure that out by himself, but if he does he'll keep quiet about it."

"Why did you tell me about Berini and your plan? You've never discussed any of your cases with me before."

"Panic."

"I beg your pardon."

"Panic," he repeated. "Because I was terribly afraid of losing you. After the way I ran away from you that night I felt I owed you a complete and thorough explanation. So I made up my mind to confide in you."

"I think that's very sweet." She gave him her most delightful smile.

"Is this the woman," he asked in wonderment, "who earlier this evening ordered put to death the whole royal line of the House of Judah, including her own grandson, and who shook her fist at heaven in defiance of God himself?"

She pretended indifference with a slight toss of her head. "A trifle," she replied. "You saw me in a bitchy mood."

They made love on Daphne's large, canopied bed, and then they fell asleep. Blanc dreamed he was face to face with Berini. He'd never seen him before, but yet he knew him at sight. They were at an inn, seated across from each other at a table. Perhaps it was the flickering firelight, the blaze that played across their faces from the open fireplace, that played tricks on Blanc's mind. But Berini's face seemed to be changing. Now he was Berini, and now he was . . . Cagliostro!

"You see, Chief Inspector, I am Alessandro, Conte Cagliostro. That is something you did not reckon into your calculations. You wish to arrest me, but how can you do so? I have already been acquitted in the affair of the Queen's Necklace. Surely you know your precious Code Napoléon."

"I'm arresting you not for the diamond necklace but for the murder of the seven people in the Rue Saint-Guillaume," he replied.

"Oh, that business!" Now the man across the table from him was Berini again. "But what can you possibly hope to prove against me? No one saw the murderer arrive or leave the house. No one saw the murders committed. Do you think your feeble witnesses will amount to anything? That coachman, or the hotel porter? Their testimony will be discounted entirely. They won't even be able to swear it was me they saw. My enemies will be made a laughingstock, exactly as last time. For, you see, I can change my appearance. Here, let me show you."

He played with the diamond stickpin in his cravat and held it at such an angle that it caught the reflection of the firelight. It glowed and blazed with a brightness such as Blanc had never before seen in his life. A beam of light from the diamond shone directly into his eyes. It blinded him with its unbearable whiteness, with a heat so intense that it became a freezing chill. It pierced his eyes, right through their sockets and into his brain. His skull was aflame. . . .

He awoke in a cold sweat and found Daphne leaning over him. "I . . . I had a nightmare," he said.

"I know."

"I dreamed I arrested Berini. But he was Cagliostro. He kept changing from one to the other, and then he tricked me."

"I'll be very happy," Daphne Perrault remarked, wiping his brow with a lace kerchief, "when this case of yours against Berini is finished."

He sighed heavily. "So will I, Daphne. So will I."

On Wednesday, October 28, a messenger came around to

Blanc from M. Lenoir. Blanc broke the seal, read the short note, and immediately went across the street to the Ministry of Police to see Fouché. The Minister's assistant, Devereaux, indicated to him that his chief was alone in his office. Blanc knocked and entered the chamber.

Fouché looked up from his work at his Chief Inspector, who said only two words: "He's accepted."

CHAPTER 11

There was a question that had been bothering Blanc in the event that Berini might accept his invitation. Now that he had accepted, he needed to reach a decision. He had, as he saw it, one of two choices: He could either wait until his man reached Paris and then place him under arrest, or he could arrest him as soon as he crossed the border. Each had certain disadvantages.

Berini's senses were highly developed, far more so than those of most people. If, upon entering France, or anywhere along his route to Paris, he sensed or felt or smelled that something was wrong, he would turn around, recross the border, and be lost to Blanc forever. That was a real possibility, and one that Blanc couldn't afford to discount.

The alternative, then, was to arrest him at the border. The question was, which border? If he was coming from Vienna he had a choice of four border stations: Basle, Mulhouse, Sarrebruck and Strasbourg. Any farther north or south would really be going out of his way.

So far, Blanc had been "chasing" his adversary mainly while sitting behind his desk—the first time in his entire career that he had handled a case that way. Some instinct told him he could no longer afford to go on playing the master manipulator working his set of puppets. In a way, he had Marais to thank for that; the journalist had very nearly upset his plans. He didn't want anything else to go wrong, and there were too many things that could go wrong.

He sent for his inspectors—Cartier, Morel, Dourouflé, Delmotte, LaFarge, Richard, Terrell, and Bastard—to brief them and give them their assignments. They stood or sat around the Chief Inspector's office, each of them knowing that this was their most important case yet, the one in which the Emperor had taken a personal interest, and that the success or failure of its outcome might depend on him personally.

The short, stout Ddouroufflé, who had the best sense of humor there, excepting only the Chief himself, couldn't resist looking around the room and remarking, "There are enough of us here to form a police choir. Shall we begin with the 'Chant du départ'?"

They all laughed, including Blanc.

"Let's get down to business first. If, afterward, you all feel like standing up and singing, I have no objection. I might even join you, but I warn you we'll only have time for one song. M. Berini has accepted our invitation. He may well be on his way to Paris already."

He detailed his reasons for wanting to grab Berini at the border crossing, and pointed out that it would involve the utmost alertness on each man's part. He was sending Morel and Douroufflé to Basle, Delmotte and LaFarge to Mulhouse, and Terrell and Richard to Sarrebruck. He and Bastard would go to Strasbourg.

To Cartier would go the dubious honor of staying in Paris and taking charge of the department in his absence. (He caught the momentary look of disappointment on Cartier's face, but he knew the Breton would realize the necessity of the assignment. As it was, he was denuding the city of its best inspectors.)

He gave them again the physical description of Berini, which they all knew. The border guards were to have his description as well as the name, and they were to summon the inspectors immediately in the event of his arrival. The inspectors, of course, were always to be available at a moment's notice.

"Wouldn't that make him suspicious, Chief?" LaFarge asked.

"You mean, being asked to wait a few moments? I don't think so. There are often delays at the border."

"What if he should come in by another way altogether?" Richard ventured.

"Then, it will be up to Cartier to arrest him once he registers at the Baudoins. That, presumably, is where he would be staying again if he reached Paris. But why should he come back stealthily?" Blanc added. "There's no reason for him to do so, any more than there is for him to use another name. If he's coming back to France, that means he suspects nothing."

He then proceeded to give them a description of animal magnetism, as best he understood it. He gave them explicit instructions about what to do and what not to do in the event that Berini should try to put them into a trance.

"That is the only weapon he has," he concluded, "so don't let yourselves be taken in. And now, gentlemen, you have one hour to get home and pack before you leave Paris. The coaches M. Fouché has so kindly requisitioned for us will be waiting in front of your houses at. . . ." He took out his gold watch. "At a quarter past eleven. I wish you all good luck and good hunting."

Blanc went across to see Fouché again. He had sent Alphonse ahead to tell Émil to pack his things. He himself would take a cab home. He had also written out a note for Émil to take around to Daphne after his departure.

"So, Chief Inspector," the Minister said, "everything's prepared, is it?"

"Yes, M. le Ministre. My men have been dispatched and dispersed. I'm taking young Bastard with me to Strasbourg, and the rest is in the hands of God."

"What an odd thing to say!" the former seminarian remarked. "I know it's become fashionable to go to church again, but do you really believe that?"

"Yes, I do. In this case and in every other I've ever had. Perhaps more so this time."

"Yes, there are so many possibilities. One of them—and I'm sure you've thought of this—is that your men might arrest Berini and he might get away from them."

"A very real possibility," Blanc agreed. "The man is unique, and they've never been up against anyone like him before. Neither, for that matter, have I. But he's still only a human being, not a god. He's capable of making a mistake, and so are we. Therefore—"

"It's all in the hands of God." The Minister stood up and extended his hand. "Good luck, Blanc."

Basle is a German Protestant city, and both Morel and Doupouflé were French Catholics. They understandably felt ill at ease there, as well as bored and homesick. Erasmus, Calvin, Holbein the Younger, Euler, and the Bernoullis had lived and worked there, but as the two inspectors had never heard of any of them, Basle was, for them, merely a strange town and an inhospitable one. In point of fact, Douroufflé had heard of Calvin, but only as a sort of bogeyman used by priests to threaten rebellious small boys (although it had been that ogre Martin Luther who had haunted his childhood dreams). He probably didn't associate the man with the city.

The two men stayed at a small inn across the square from the customs house and spent all their time alternating between those two points. They shared a small room, ate food they were unaccustomed to, and couldn't get their favorite wine. At night they played cards.

"I'm sure you realize," Morel said to his colleague one night, "that the Chief picked the most likely crossing point for himself. Strasbourg is almost on a direct line from Vienna."

"Of course," Douroufflé replied, "but it wasn't to grab off the glory. You know that if one of us arrested Berini we'd get the credit, and our names would appear in the papers. The Chief has never been vain."

Morel had to agree with that.

"Besides," Douroufflé went on, "isn't he entitled to it? Both the credit and the best spot, I mean. He knew the murderer's name and motive before the rest of us were aware of his existence. He even traced him to his home city. The street, the house, the very door."

Again Morel was forced to agree. "He may have some strange ideas—though not when it comes to women—but he's a good policeman, no question about that."

Douroufflé leaned forward, but not so far that his companion could see his cards. "Don't you see? The Chief sees this as a personal contest, a duel between himself and Berini. You know, I have the feeling he's not so much eager to arrest him as he is to meet him."

"In that case," Morel suggested, "why didn't he just take a trip to Vienna and knock at his door? It would have been a lot easier on everyone, especially on us. We wouldn't have to be sitting in this Godforsaken place."

Douroufié shrugged. "Oh, I don't know. It's not so bad. It might even be tolerable, if one could speak the language, keep down the food, drink their wine, and stand the people."

He threw his cards down on the table. "*Trente-et-quarante*," he said triumphantly.

Sarrebruck, too, was a German city, the old capital of the counts of Nassau-Saarbrücken, until it was occupied by the French in 1793. Richard had been there before, when he was a captain in the Army. The place was exactly as he remembered it, as seen from a soldier's point of view: a small provincial city with a limited social life. That had consisted mainly of drinking, occasional duels, and exercising their horses.

This time he didn't even have the diversion of those amenities. The morose, taciturn Terrell was not much company. He spoke mainly in monosyllables, and then only when spoken to. Richard didn't really know the man, and felt they had nothing in common.

Terrell was a policeman one learned to respect through familiarity and shared experiences. His thin features, with his long, perennially red nose, sad eyes, and rather big ears, and his long, thin frame were admittedly not prepossessing. But anyone who had ever seen him run unheedingly through a cross fire to rescue a wounded policeman and then look around in amazement at the suggestion that he'd done a brave thing, knew his value. He was also dogged and tenacious in his work.

They were both standing at the city gates, only a few yards from the guard shack.

"Do you think he'll come this way?" Richard asked, just for the sake of making conversation.

"He's got to get there some way," Terrell replied. He also hardly ever used proper nouns, either for people or places. What he presumably meant was that Berini had, somehow, to get from Vienna to Paris or, more specifically, from number 237 The Graben to the new Hotel Baudoins in the Carrousel.

"It's funny," Richard said, talking more to himself than his companion, "when I was here last, fifteen years ago, I'd look for a fight—any excuse to challenge someone to a duel, or have him challenge me—just to break the boredom. Now I'm not even tempted."

He stuck his thumbs into his belt and surveyed the scene: the medieval-looking city sitting in the afternoon sunlight, with the spires of the Ludwigskirche rising into the blue sky. "Of course," he went on, "I was younger then. But mainly I think it's having a wife and a couple of children that takes that out of you. Are you married?"

"Yes," Terrell replied simply. He offered no further information. Richard could imagine the witty, volatile conversations he and his wife must have at home.

"Any children?"

"Three," Terrell said. If they resembled their father physically, Richard hoped to God they were boys and not girls. He had a mental picture of three little Terrells at home, of varying sizes, all with long thin faces, red noses, and big ears.

"I'm going to the inn for a beer," Richard announced. "You won't mind staying here alone for a while?"

"No," Terrell said. Left alone, he, too, studied the scene, which he found not unattractive. Nevertheless, he wished he was back in Paris with Annie and the children and holding down his regular beat.

Delmotte and LaFarge had worked together as a team many times before. They worked well together, perhaps because their personalities were so different. The swarthy Delmotte had a Mediterranean temperament; he was volatile, quick-tempered, and brave to the point of foolhardiness. Like most men from his region, he had a tendency to swagger. LaFarge, on the other hand, was a quiet, reflective family man who puffed contemplatively on his pipe while he thought a problem through. He was generally well liked and respected by his colleagues.

It was at LaFarge's instigation that they actually rehearsed their arrest of Berini.

"Why?" Delmotte had protested. "We've arrested lots of people."

"Berini isn't lots of people." LaFarge puffed quietly away. "He's unique. You heard the Chief say it, and if you doubt his word just remember that he put seven people to sleep and then slit their throats. If we're not careful, he'll carve two more notches into his walking stick, and we'll be condemned to lie in this backwater hole through all eternity. They won't even bring our bodies back to Paris for a military burial, nor would we deserve one."

"Then, how would you go about arresting him?" Delmotte flung forth the challenge.

LaFarge blew out a great cloud of blue smoke. "First of all, we'll do what the Chief suggested: take away his weapons—his diamond stickpin and his gold watch. We'll give him a signed receipt for them if he insists. Then one or another of us is always to be awake, even if he's sleeping. He may only be pretending sleep."

"Why don't we give him a smoke of your pipe?" Delmotte suggested. "Then he'll be unconscious all the way from here to Paris—if he's still alive."

"All right," LaFarge said. "Let's suppose that I'm Berini and you're the one on duty, or the guard summoned you. What would you do?"

"The most dangerous weapon you've got is that pipe, and I almost wish you were Berini, so that I could take it away from you."

"Joking aside, how would you handle it?"

"M. Berini, in the name of the Emperor and of the French Empire. . . ."

In truth, there was little else for the two men to do. Mulhouse was the smallest, least attractive, and least interesting of the border cities. All of them—Morel, Dourouflé, Richard, Terrell, as well as Delmotte and LaFarge—secretly envied Cartier, who was frolicking in Paris and who, for his part, was disappointed because he was missing the action.

For centuries, Strasbourg had been a haven of refuge for political exiles and victims of religious persecution. Louis XIV had seized the free city for France; yet even after the annexation, when Protestants were persecuted in France after 1685, the persecution didn't extend into Strasbourg. To Blanc, who was familiar with the city, the magnificent Rhenish cathedral, with its single spire rising ever upward toward heaven, stood as a symbol of the city's freedom and tolerance.

A Roman Catholic cathedral in a city that had embraced the Reformation and been a member of the Protestant League, and with one of the oldest Protestant universities in Europe. A city that had accepted the Revolution but joined in none of its excesses.

Blanc had pointed out the sights to Bastard upon their arrival, as their coach drove through the town. Thereafter, like the other inspectors, they stayed pretty close to the customs house.

Assistant Inspector Bastard admired his Chief greatly. He thought it nothing short of miraculous that Blanc had discovered the identity of the man Berini.

"Do you think he'll come through this way, Chief Inspector?"

Blanc gave much the same reply Terrell had given Richard, albeit phrased more grammatically. Bastard may have been young and inexperienced, but he was not a fool. There was a question that had been bothering him, and he'd been debating with himself whether to voice it or not. Finally he decided that here, with the two of them alone and away from Paris, and with nothing to do all day, it wouldn't be stepping out of line.

"What happens if we don't get him at all, sir? If he changes his mind about coming back?"

Blanc couldn't resist a smile. "Do you mean, what happens to Berini? Or to Léon the Frog? To the Paris police, or to me personally?"

Bastard blushed. "Well, all of them."

"Obviously Berini's safe as long as he never touches French soil. Léon the Frog will be released under any circumstances. I have M. Fouché's word on that, and he has never broken his word to me yet. I personally would want to make a clean breast of it and give the papers the entire story, but I rather suspect our Minister will release Léon on the condition that he live elsewhere under a different name and never return to Paris again. Poor fellow," he added, "that's a death sentence for Léon right there."

"And the police?" Bastard prompted. Blanc knew perfectly well what he meant. Young Bastard was intelligent enough to figure out for himself that the Chief Inspector had gambled with his career.

"Whatever the outcome, the Paris police will have covered themselves with glory. If it was Léon, we got him three days after the murders were committed. If it was Berini, we lured him back to France and captured him against all the odds.

"As for the Chief Inspector of the Criminal Investigation Department, he can probably weather the storm if we don't get Berini. Everyone in a public position makes enemies, and they're always waiting for him to make a mistake. It's not inconceivable that my enemies may get hold of the true facts, but I don't think they'll dare contradict the official story."

He realized that the report of his little confrontation with Prefect Dubois had made the rounds of the entire department. He no longer cared what Dubois discovered for himself; he'd have to keep quiet about it or incur the Emperor's disfavor. If his plan didn't work, there would always be some among those who knew the real story, like Marais and Dubois, who would believe that Léon the Frog had merely been used to save the Chief Inspector's reputation. They could never be convinced that Blanc had meant to set a trap with him to capture the real murderer.

To hell with them! Had they been in his place, they would have used Léon to save their reputations—and really executed him. If Dante were living in France in the nineteenth century, he would have set aside a special circle in hell for the likes of Armand, Pardon, Desmans, Selvay, and Dubois. There they could take turns betraying each other through all eternity.

"Shall I tell you what really bothers me?" he said to Bastard. "It is that one of our teams will capture Berini and that he will escape. That would really make us look like fools and would be devilishly difficult to cover up."

"Would the men responsible for letting him escape be discharged?"

"I hope not," Blanc replied, with a twinkle in his eye. "It might be us. Besides, I don't think it's fair to drum them out or even ask them to resign. Berini's powers are unique, probably in all of Europe."

"You did give us a briefing, sir."

"I'm afraid it wasn't much of a briefing. The truth is, my young friend, that we don't have any idea of the extent of Berini's powers."

Blanc was correct in several of the things he surmised. Fouché had indeed decided to exile Léon from Paris if his Chief Inspector's plan fell through. It was true that he and his men had no idea of the full extent of Berini's powers. What he didn't realize was that neither, in fact, did Berini. Animal magnetism, or mesmerism as it was later to be called, was a new and unexplored concept.

On Saturday, November 7, at 7:30 in the evening, as darkness was already descending over the city of Strasbourg, a handsome gilt-framed carriage drawn by two fine horses pulled up at the city gates in front of the customs house. One of the two guards on duty at the time was an alert young Strasbourger named Cramer. As soon as he caught sight of the carriage's elegant occupant, he slipped out to summon the Chief Inspector, not waiting for an identification.

CHAPTER 12

Young Cramer was not an alarmist. It turned out that he was right. By the time Blanc got to the shack—and that was only about three minutes later—the other guard had made a definite identification.

Blanc didn't need it. One look at the occupant of the carriage told him he had the right man. In the light of the oil lamp the guard was holding, he saw the handsome, well-formed face, the deep-set, visionary eyes, the elegant cut of the clothes. He even spotted the diamond stickpin (which, it seemed, he always wore) and the mahogany walking stick with its ivory handle.

"M. Berini," he said quietly, "in the name of the Emperor and of the French Empire I arrest you for the murder of the seven people at number 16 Rue Saint-Guillaume."

A subtle change of expression came over Berini's face. Was that a fleeting look of fear in his eyes, or had the Chief Inspector imagined it?

A long time seemed to elapse before Berini spoke. "A trap," he said.

"Yes, a trap," Blanc replied. "Please step out of the carriage, and leave your walking stick behind. My assistant, as you see, has a pistol trained on you, and one of the guards has a pistol trained on your man up there on the box."

"You, come down," the guard with the lantern called out to the coachman. The man merely looked confused.

"*Du, komm 'runter,*" Cramer said.

"*Komm doch herunter, Karl,*" Berini said as he stepped out of the carriage. "*Es wird dir nichts geschehen.*"

Then, to the Chief Inspector: "On my word, Karl knows

nothing about it. I don't think he's even read the stories in the papers. He's been my coachman for five years."

He spoke French with an ever so slight accent, probably assumed at first, when he took on his new identity, but ingrained by now after years of living in Austria.

"Even if he knew all about it," Blanc remarked, "his connection with the murders would be virtually impossible to prove. But we'll need him to give testimony in court."

"You sound pretty confident," Berini observed.

"I am. Let's go to the inn, though. It's only two streets from here, and you must be hungry. I know I am."

"Are you Inspector Blanc?"

"Yes."

"I've read about you. It's strange: I've often wanted to meet you."

"And I, for the past six weeks, have been wanting to meet you. Now it appears that we are stuck with each other's company from here all the way to Paris." He gave Bastard instructions to take the coachman to the local prefecture and have him put in a cell overnight. Then the young inspector was to join them at the inn. On their way through the already dark streets, Blanc walked behind Berini and kept his own pistol pointed directly at the center of his back. He neither asked for nor received his prisoner's word that he wouldn't try to escape.

The inn, L'Homme Libre, was already well filled, both with locals and visitors who were passing through on their way into or out of the French Empire. Blanc motioned Berini over to his regular table, which the *patron* held for him each evening. Seeing his two distinguished guests together, that worthy hurried over to their table.

"Good evening, Chief Inspector," he said. "Good evening, M. Berini. It's a pleasure to have you back with us again."

Berini made a wry face at the inspector. "Thank you, Henri," he said. "Unfortunately, I can't return the compliment this time."

"May I recommend," the *patron* said, "our goose à la Strasbourg. It's our finest dish, and we have some superb geese which were freshly slaughtered this afternoon."

"Indeed," Berini observed. "How appropriate! That sounds fine to me. And you, Inspector Blanc?"

Blanc nodded in agreement.

"And a bottle of your best Riesling. Do you still have that fine vintage I drank when I stayed here three months ago?"

"Yes, M. Berini. Inspector." He hurried off to get the wine.

"Before we get down to any further pleasantries," Blanc said, "let me tell you that Inspector Bastard is coming here with a detachment of men from the local prefecture. They will keep this inn surrounded all night, and they have orders to shoot to kill should you try to escape."

"Really?" Berini raised his eyebrows quizzically. "Are they good shots?"

"I haven't the faintest idea, but one of them might be lucky."

"Yes, that's a strong possibility," Berini agreed. "My chances of escape are admittedly extremely slim. On the other hand, what would you say my chances are if I reach Paris?"

"There's evidence against you, quite obviously, or I wouldn't have prepared such an elaborate trap. You'll stand trial, but as for the outcome . . . one never knows."

"Doesn't one? Won't the judges be instructed to find me guilty? I would think the outcome is a foregone conclusion."

"No, M. Berini, not any more. That day is gone in France—forever, I hope. If you plead innocent, and with a good lawyer, there is always a chance that you'll walk out of the courtroom a free man."

The Free Man, Blanc said to himself. The name of this inn. He was certain the same thought had crossed Berini's mind.

"Should that happen," he continued, "there will always be two people, you and I, who know you're really guilty. But I am hoping that you will confess."

The *patron* came over with a bottle of wine and two glasses, and at that moment Bastard came into the room. He caught his Chief's eye and came over to their table.

"The coachman is under lock and key, Chief Inspector, and the inn is surrounded."

"Splendid, Bastard. Why don't you take a chair and join us." He motioned the patron back to their table and ordered another glass and another bottle of Riesling. "We're having goose, freshly slaughtered. How does that suit you?"

Young Bastard, who was somewhat taken aback by the entire event, could only nod his assent. Following his report, he kept quiet and let the other two men talk. Although he followed their conversation avidly, he had the feeling, which increased as the evening wore on, that they had forgotten his presence.

"Why on earth should I confess?" Berini picked up the thread of their conversation.

"Because you killed their wives."

Berini looked at his captor with genuine surprise. "You are either the greatest policeman in all Europe, or the most naïve idealist I've ever met."

"Possibly both."

"Whatever happened to that fellow you arrested for the murders?"

"Léon the Frog? He'll be released as soon as we get to Paris."

"Then, there was no trial or execution."

"No."

"And no offer from the Cirque."

"M. Lenoir wrote that letter, but I dictated it. We had to take him into our confidence."

Berini knew how to accept defeat with grace. He smiled. "Your reputation is well deserved, Inspector Blanc, and you really study your man carefully. But, as we'd never met, what did you base your study of me on?"

"Ecclesiastes."

For a brief moment, Berini seemed puzzled. Then he understood. "Ah, yes. 'Vanity of vanities, all is vanity.' How appropriate, and how true! I presume we start for Paris in the morning."

Blanc nodded.

"Why didn't you put me in a cell?"

"It's easier to talk here. Certainly a lot more pleasant. You are from Toulon."

It was a statement, rather than a question, and caused Berini to regard his adversary with even greater respect. "How did you reach that conclusion?"

"That was the only connection between the four men, the only time they'd ever been together in the same place before they lived in Paris."

"As long as you've told me so much—and remember, I admit nothing—why don't you tell me why I killed them."

"I would think that's pretty obvious, M. Berini. Everyone knows what happened in Toulon. I'm under no obligation to do this, but I'm going to tell you what evidence we have against you. Then you can decide whether you want to confess. Whether, after all these years, you finally want to rid yourself of this burden that's been weighing upon your heart."

"Then," the other said, not without some sarcasm, "I will be a free man."

"No," Blanc replied gravely, "but you'll be a cleansed one. For seventeen years you've lived for nothing but revenge. Now that you've achieved it, and been caught, why not make a clean breast of it? I think we've got enough evidence against you to get a conviction, but I'll let you decide that for yourself."

"That sounds fair enough. But here comes our host, assisted by his waiter, carrying what really does look like a magnificent bird. Confessions were not meant to be made over sumptuous meals. We'll have plenty of opportunity to resume this discussion. Incidentally, have you tried this Riesling? It really is a splendid wine. *À votre santé, messieurs.*"

"*À votre santé*, M. Berini."

After dinner, in Blanc's room, and again in Bastard's silent presence, the two men resumed their discussion.

"You were going to tell me what evidence you had against me."

"Quite so. First and foremost, you are the chief witness against yourself. Your bizarre and unique manner of slaughtering your victims pinpoints you as the murderer. There's not another man on the whole Continent who could put a roomful of people to sleep. Unless you can establish your presence elsewhere at the time of the murders—and we both know you can't —that is the most damning piece of evidence we have."

Berini was silent and let Blanc continue.

"We know what time the murders were committed—not precisely, of course, but sometime after eleven in the morning, when the servants left the house, and half past two in the afternoon, when a coachman named Marcel Jonell picked you up on the Rue Saint-Dominique. He told us, without any prompting, that you were walking in the same direction he was going. That is, *away* from the Rue Saint-Guillaume. He took you to the Hotel Baudoins, where your coach was waiting for you, trunks strapped on and all, for an extremely hasty departure. The porter, Édouard, related how you pressed some money into his hand instead of taking a more formal and dignified leave."

Berini looked at Blanc expectantly, as though he were waiting for more.

"That's all there is," the Chief Inspector told him. "I told you I was being absolutely fair with you and, Léon the Frog and the Cirque offer notwithstanding, I have no further tricks up my sleeve."

"If I can believe you," Berini said, "and there's no reason why I should, you are telling me that you set this elaborate trap for me on the basis of those three points?"

"We've caught murderers on slenderer threads than that."

"Were they convicted?"

"Sometimes. Not always. I'm a policeman, M. Berini. Unlike you, I'm not a judge, jury, and executioner all rolled into one. I don't pass judgment on people, and my job ends when I've made my arrest. Thereafter, our able prosecutor takes over."

"And, of course, my confession would make your triumph in this case complete."

"Yes," Blanc agreed, "I'm honest enough to admit that. But I won't die of grief if I don't get it. Consider the case the Empire has against you. Your only defense, as I see it, is to keep shouting coincidence.

"Point one. Seven people in a room were put into a trance before they were butchered. You are the only person in Europe with that unique ability, the power to put a roomful of people into a trance, and you were in Paris at the time. Coincidence? Very well, I grant you a jury might well go along with the first one.

"Point two. A coachman picked you up one street from the house where the murders were committed at the time of day they were committed. You were headed toward the Rue des Saints Pères when he saw you—in other words, you were taking the direction away from the house. Coincidence? You'll have a much harder time making a jury believe that one.

"Point three. The coachman took you to the Hotel Baudoins, where your man already had your trunks strapped to your coach, all set for a fast departure. 'Escape' is the word the prosecutor will use. Coincidence?

"You're entitled to your opinion, M. Berini, but I don't think your lawyer will pull it off."

Berini still said nothing.

"There is one more thing: the matter of a motive. Surely we can find someone in Toulon who remembers you. You can't have changed that much in seventeen years."

Berini was quiet for a long time, and Blanc kept still, to let his words sink in. Bastard, who was seated at the door, was fascinated by the whole thing. Ever since he'd entered the inn earlier that evening, he'd had the feeling of being a spectator at a medieval joust. And the opponents, he thought, were quite evenly matched.

There was a long silence. Both antagonists sat in chairs facing each other, a few meters apart. Berini, in his elegant clothes, continued to look unruffled. He and the Chief Inspector might have been discussing the weather or the town's architecture.

"Wouldn't it have been easier for you to place the blame on—"

"Léon the Frog."

"The papers said he's a criminal."

"He has a police record."

"Why didn't you try him?"

"Because he didn't do it. Léon's never killed anyone in his life."

"You talk as though you like him."

"I do. Admittedly, he went into that house to steal, but in the first place he doesn't have the ability to put people to sleep. Secondly, he was seen leaving there hours after they were killed. And third, he didn't steal anything. What was he doing there all that time, keeping the corpses company?"

"Again, three points," Berini observed.

"Three is supposed to be a mystic number, isn't it?"

"You're not a Mason?"

"No."

"I am. So was Mozart, who lived on the same street I do, and so is my teacher, Dr. Mesmer. But I forgot, in France Catholics can't be Masons. You are Catholic?"

"Yes."

"Do you believe in God?"

"I'm not sure. But I do believe in man. And God, if he exists, must believe in man."

"You are an idealist!" Berini said. "So you really think I'll confess by the time we reach Paris?"

"I'm certain of it."

"Will it save my life?"

"No, but it will save your soul. Besides, you don't really think you can win in court. Rightly or wrongly, for good or evil, you've done what you felt you had to. Why not own up to it? Why play the clown, the fool, telling story after story that you don't really expect anyone to believe?"

"In other words, why not go to the guillotine with dignity."

"When it comes down to it," Blanc agreed, "yes. Why not?"

"Would you? Go to the guillotine with dignity, I mean?"

"If I had to, I hope I would have the courage to do just that. Do you know what the great irony in this whole case is?"

"That I let myself be caught?" Berini suggested.

"No. The irony is that, if you hadn't killed their wives, you might have made a full confession and walked out of the courtroom a free man anyway."

"Do you really believe that?" Berini sounded incredulous. "They were important men."

"They were murderers," Blanc said. "I rather suspect one of them had regrets about it afterward. Not that that changes anything."

"I'm sure the shades of their victims would be pleased to learn that," Berini said with heavy irony. "A bloodbath, and one of them had regrets!"

There followed another lengthy silence. Both men—policeman and murderer, captor and prisoner—sat quietly at ease, regarding one another. The tensest person in the room by far was young Bastard, who sat nervously in his chair in front of the closed door. He had an intense feeling that something was about to happen. Something momentous.

And it did.

"When the Republican troops marched into our city of Toulon," Berini began quietly, "the populace had mixed feelings about them. Some of the people we knew personally welcomed them with genuine enthusiasm. Others of our friends and neighbors, Royalists, feared the worst. It didn't make a bit of difference. The Republicans slaughtered indiscriminately. Every day, they would take one hundred men, march them to the central square, and shoot them. They simply grabbed whoever happened to be on the street. After the first few days, when people caught on, they stayed off the streets at midday. The soldiers then came into the houses and dragged men out.

"I didn't hide under the bed or in the attic, but somehow I managed to escape. They took my brother, but they left me alone. He was nineteen at the time, a brilliant student who would have made a first-rate surgeon. I was three years younger than he. They marched him and the other men to the square, had them stand with their hands clasped behind their necks, and then shot them down. My parents tried to stop me, but I insisted on going to the square. I wanted to see who his executioners were.

"I memorized their faces. It wasn't difficult to learn their names afterward. There I was, a sixteen-year-old boy, trembling with impotent rage, swearing to take revenge on his brother's murderers. I'm sure that, had they known about it, those butchers would merely have laughed. But I took an oath, then and there, that if I lived I would avenge my brother's death if it took me the rest of my life to do it.

"Even as a sixteen-year-old, I wasn't naïve. I realized I couldn't get even with every soldier in the company, but they weren't important. Most of them would probably be killed in battle anyway. It was the men who gave the orders, the ones in charge I was after. I never did find out if this was true, but the rumor circulating around the city was that the general in charge resigned in protest. If it is true, then more honor to him. But public executions were ordered by the two people's representatives who were attached to every army. According to the law, one people's representative had to be present at each execution. Both of them were there that day."

"Pardon and Desmans," Blanc said.

"Yes, Pardon and Desmans. Isn't that ironic, gentlemen? A butcher of innocent people named Pardon! There was no pardon or mercy shown in Toulon. The lieutenant in charge of the execution was Armand. The sergeant who carried out his order was Selvay. Those were the four I was determined to get.

"After about a week of this, they erected a guillotine. Thereafter the killings became more 'methodical': they only beheaded Royalists. In most cases, people whose neighbors had informed on them. And there were many who informed, in the hope of saving their own skins. Most of those beheaded probably were Royalist sympathizers, but they were also largely harmless.

"I was sick of the Revolution, and of France. Two years later, I went to Geneva to study medicine. No doubt it was my brother's unfulfilled ambition that influenced me. When France annexed Geneva, I went to Vienna. There I met Dr. Mesmer and came under his tutelage. In truth, I became his prize pupil. He was, as you know, a physician, and he originally developed the theory of animal magnetism as a tool in the practice of medicine. But when he became celebrated, he also became, in effect, a showman, giving demonstrations before gatherings that could hardly be called professional.

"I decided to go my teacher one better, and became a performer, pure and simple. I played in circuses, in theaters, before fraternal organizations and in the salons of society. I gave myself an Italian name and a mysterious background. That is what fascinates people and attracts the public. Through it all I never lost sight of my goal: revenge on my brother's murderers. I realized I could use my unique power, as you called it, to gain my revenge. But in order to do that I would have to return to France. I did so, three years ago, for the first time in twelve years.

"It was largely an exploratory trip. I made discreet inquiries and, much to my surprise, had little trouble tracking my four men down. Desmans was a prominent Paris lawyer, and Armand had moved to Paris after he left the Army. Selvay was a Parisian by birth, something I hadn't known before, and had taken over his family business. I went to their addresses, stood across the street, and studied the comings and goings at their houses.

"Can you imagine how I felt, gentlemen? Seeing these men after so many years, now with wives and families, comfortable, successful, with fine houses, servants, carriages. Yet it seemed to me as though I were sixteen again, standing at the edge of the central square on a cold, sunny day, looking directly at the faces of the men who gave the command to fire. There were one hundred human beings herded together, forced to stand with their hands clasped behind their necks, and do you know what I saw on the faces of my four butchers? Hate? Joy? Not even that much. Just unconcern.

"I saw Pardon's house, but I knew he was in Sardinia. I gave a number of demonstrations at several Paris salons, but I knew the time was not yet ripe. It was enough, this time, that I had tracked them down. I knew where to find them, and they would not escape me."

"One of them almost did," Blanc observed. "Armand had a bad heart."

"Really?" Berini said, with genuine interest. "I didn't know that. It wouldn't have made any difference to me, but it was accommodating of him to wait for me. Otherwise, I would have felt cheated.

"The rest I think you know. On July twenty-first of this year I returned to Paris. My relatively modest success last time was as nothing compared to my triumphs in the leading salons of your fair city. I was lionized; everyone wanted me, and that included, *mirabile dictu*, Mme. Pardon. For Ambassador Pardon, ex-People's Representative Pardon, was back in Paris, and so I had all four of my butchers where I wanted them.

"I did more than score a social success this time. I gave myself a reputation for temperament that I don't think any tenor or prima donna at the Opéra could have equaled. I insisted on seeing the hostess' guest list, insisted on having approval of who attended my demonstrations, and pulled tantrums if I didn't get my way. The ladies seemed to find it endearing. They smiled, as at an unruly child, and gave in to me. Some were so desperate to have me in their salons I think they would have given in to the most outrageous demands, even to setting their mothers-in-law on fire!

"By the time I fulfilled my last engagement, Mme. Pardon knew exactly what to expect. And finally the day arrived: the day I'd been awaiting for seventeen years. The boy who'd stood at the edge of the square seventeen years before was seated at the table with the four butchers who'd murdered his brother. The others ate like pigs, but I had to make a pretense of eating and try to keep my excitement down. That meal seemed interminable. Finally it was over, and the moment I had waited and planned and prayed for had arrived. We all got up from the table, the ladies preceded us, and I followed my four butchers into the drawing room."

CHAPTER 13

The following morning at seven, the little company set out for Paris. Blanc, Berini, and Bastard sat in the Chief Inspector's coach, with Alphonse presiding up on his box. An inspector and two policemen, borrowed from the local prefecture, followed with Karl in Berini's coach. Blanc and Berini had talked till the early hours of the morning; then they tried to get some sleep, with Blanc and Bastard taking turns standing guard over their prisoner. The inspector on watch literally stood, to keep from falling asleep, pistol in hand.

Blanc was seated next to Berini, and Bastard sat facing them. It was a chilly, overcast day, and a sharp drizzle had started to fall as they stepped into the coach. Looking out the window as they drove away from the city, they could barely make out the famous spire of the cathedral reaching toward heaven as though exhorting man to free himself of his earthly hates and prejudices.

"I always liked Strasbourg," Berini remarked.

"So do I," Blanc said.

"The difference is that you'll see it again and I won't."

"I still don't understand," said Blanc, reverting to their previous night's discussion, "how you managed to get just those four men, and no others, to Mme. Pardon's affair."

Berini couldn't help smiling at the reminiscence. "You can believe me, it wasn't easy. The poor lady had quite a list drawn up. I told you about my hard-won reputation for artistic temperament, bordering on and sometimes surpassing arrogance. I complained that these people and those had already seen my demonstrations. In some cases, that was true. Others were unacceptable to me for one or another reason: known antipathy toward scientific experimentation, unsympathetic magnetism, and so on.

"I had made it a point to have present, at my previous performances, an objective, impersonal observer, usually a member of one of the professions, to attest that my subjects were really asleep and that no trickery was involved. I told Mme. Pardon that I wanted such a person in attendance this time. As a rule, this was a physician or a scientist, but a keen, analytical mind was what was most important. I had heard, I said, that Maître Desmans was the best trial lawyer in Paris. Perhaps he might be interested; did they know him?

"Mme. Pardon confessed to me that M. Desmans and her husband had once been close friends. There had been a rift between them a few years ago, but they had, of late, patched things up. They were no longer close but they were, at least, on speaking terms. She jumped at my suggestion that this might be a good way to bring them together again—that was, if her husband had no objection.

"Armand was on her list, so that was settled. It seems he'd been promoted several times before he left the Army, and in civilian life he'd gotten quite rich. Unlike Desmans and Pardon, he was not an 'educated' man. He was a self-made man, of the kind who are admitted to the best salons since the Revolution. He and Pardon had become friends since Armand came to Paris, and I understand Pardon was helpful in making contacts for him.

"My fourth butcher presented more of a problem. Selvay was not, strictly speaking, in the same social class; a member of the bourgeoisie, really. I doubt whether either Pardon or Desmans had had any contact with him since Toulon. Here I had to tread cautiously. I told Mme. Pardon that a M. and Mme. Selvay had approached me in the Tuileries and asked if I were not the Great Berini. We had gotten into a conversation. . . .

"In short, the lady was so eager to have me that she agreed to each and every one of my demands, however reluctantly. She was, of course, disappointed that I had cut her guest list so drastically: only seven people, including herself and her husband. I understood how she felt, and even sympathized with her. Here she had wanted to make a great social splash in Paris, after having been tucked away for three years in unfashionable Sardinia. I mollified her somewhat by offering to reduce my customary fee—upon her sacred promise that she would never, never divulge this fact to a living soul.

"On the other hand, I hinted broadly, all Paris would still know that Berini had performed at her house, before a select group of people. In a way, we both kept our promises, didn't we?"

"In a way," Blanc agreed. "And the servants?"

"Another of my demands. Not at all difficult, as they weren't really needed. They had prepared a cold repast, and then been given the rest of the day off."

"Why did you kill the women?" Blanc said.

"Believe me—and you must believe me—if there had been a way to exclude them from that gathering I would have done so. What could I do, tell the men not to bring their wives, one of whom was the hostess? I think Pardon was already getting suspicious. I dared not go one step further."

"You could have spared their wives," Blanc suggested.

"Is that your idea of sparing them? You were in that room. Now imagine the women waking up and finding seated next to them those horrible things that had once been their husbands. At least one woman would have spent the rest of her days in a lunatic asylum.

"The women of Toulon were not spared, Inspector Blanc. True, only men were taken to the square—and boys who were not yet grown men. But God knows how many women were raped and killed by drunken, rampaging soldiers, with no attempt made to stop them. And women were guillotined. A city was raped, a French city. Not by English soldiers, or Spaniards, or Italians, or Sardinians, but by Frenchmen.

"My two distinguished, educated butchers, the lawyer and the diplomat, were there for that specific purpose, to instigate the rape and supervise it. They were accursed, and I was merely the instrument of their destruction. If their wives fell under their curse, I was unable to prevent it."

"Like the House of Atreus," Blanc suggested.

"The House of Atreus was accursed by the gods. My four butchers brought their curse upon themselves."

Their host at L'Homme Libre had provided a fine basket for their journey: meat, cheese, bread, and wine.

"I could hardly help laughing at Henri's face last night," Berini remarked, "when he finally realized I was your prisoner, and that I was the reason you'd come to Strasbourg. The poor fellow seemed more distressed than I was."

They were traveling along the Meurthe now. Their progress was necessarily slow because of the poor condition of the roads, an inheritance from the days of the Directory. They were further impeded by the steady downpour, which also severely limited their range of vision. Bastard stuck his head out the window and reported that they seemed to have lost the other coach.

"That's not surprising," Berini observed. "My horses have come all the way from Vienna, and yours are fresh. It doesn't look at though we'll reach Nancy by nightfall."

"No, we won't," Blanc replied. "We'll have to content ourselves with Lunéville."

"How is it?"

"All right, I suppose. King Stanislas was content enough there. Of course," he added, "we won't be staying at his palace. We'll be lucky if we don't spend the night in a ditch."

It had been agreed that morning between himself and the other inspector that, in the event the two parties became separated, Blanc's coach would not wait for the other. They would travel on to Paris individually. Darkness had fallen by the time they reached Lunéville, a small city, a town really, noted mainly for two things: An exiled Polish king, who had been made Duke of Lorraine, had resided there; and it was the site of an international treaty that had, in the few years since it was signed, already been broken several times by both parties.

The inn couldn't compare with the one in Strasbourg, but it did at least offer a roof over their heads and shelter from the wind and rain. The small, low-beamed public room did have a fireplace, and a crackling blaze was going when the two inspectors and their prisoner were led in by the host. Blanc experienced a vaguely uneasy feeling, the nature of which he was at a loss to understand.

The three men sat down at a small round table. Seemingly, they were the only guests at supper. If there were others, they had either eaten already and retired to their rooms, or else they were due to make a later appearance. Their host went off to see what he could get together in the way of a meal.

Blanc looked into the blazing fire, and then back at his two companions. But there are three of us here, he said to himself, when there ought to be only two.

Bastard had been wondering aloud what had happened to the other coach.

"Almost anything," Blanc replied. "They might indeed have gotten stuck in a ditch, or broken an axle; or perhaps one of the horses got lame."

It might also, he thought, be due to the difference between drivers. One of the policemen had taken the reins of Berini's coach, not Karl, and although the man doubtless had driven a hay wagon, or even a police cart, he was not an expert coachman, like his man or Berini's. On the other hand, Karl had been compensated for having to spend a night in a cell by sitting inside as a passenger—perhaps for the first time in his life.

Bastard had a pained expression on his face that both Blanc and Berini couldn't fail to notice. It was almost comical in its strained intensity.

"I saw an outhouse behind the inn as we drove up," Blanc said. "Go right ahead, Inspector, and don't worry about us. We'll be quite all right here."

Bastard murmured something inaudible, got up, and then went out, ready to brave the elements.

"He seems a conscientious young man," Berini remarked. "I gather his promotion was a recent one. Of course, his youth alone would tell me that."

Blanc nodded. Berini continued to talk in a quiet, steady tone. Although the man was, as he had found, an engaging conversationalist, Blanc had lost track of what he was saying. Berini's voice seemed to float in and out of his consciousness. Now a few words stood out, and then the words receded back to a low, steady murmur, like the rushing of the sea heard at a distance. Berini had taken out his gold watch in the most casual manner, as though he merely wished to consult the time. He dangled it in front of the Chief Inspector's eyes and then, like a pendulum, started it swinging to and fro. Tell him to put it away, Blanc said to himself, or take it away from him. But his eyelids felt so heavy, so very heavy. . . .

He was dropping into a black pit, and he mustn't let the blackness envelop him. He mustn't! He could fight against the blackness. He knew he could. But, God, he felt so tired. No, he couldn't give in. He had to stay awake. Someone had once given him a sleeping potion in a drink, and he'd known about it almost immediately. He'd told himself he had to fight against it, that he must stay awake. He'd gotten up and walked, around and around the room. Every muscle of his body had wanted to go to sleep, but he'd kept walking. He'd forced himself to stay awake. And he'd won. What he'd done once he could do again.

Turn away from that damn thing. Turn away! That's it. Now, Blanc. Now!

He shook his head, as though to clear it of cobwebs, and drew out his pistol. He pointed it directly at Berini's chest.

"M. Berini, if you don't put your toy away I shall be forced to take it away from you."

Berini smiled and put his watch away. "It was certainly worth an attempt. And it almost succeeded."

"Tell me," Blanc asked, "would you have cut my throat?"

"No, Inspector, I swear it. I would have put you to sleep and stolen away like a thief in the night."

The fire crackled and hissed in the grate. Blanc realized with a start that only a minute or two had elapsed since Bastard had left the room. He now had some idea of what it felt like to be put into a trance. Time had lost all meaning for him; a minute might have been an hour, or an eternity.

"What a pity!" Berini sighed. "Just think, had it been the other way around, had you gone to relieve yourself and your young assistant stayed here, I would have been a free man by now."

"No, a hunted one," Blanc corrected him. "Not quite the same thing. But you've just done me a favor. I've been negligent in my duties; hereafter I'll take away your watch and stickpin before we retire. You can have them back in the morning."

Bastard returned, drenched from his brief excursion. He looked anxious, and had obviously hurried back as quickly as he could. It was with a palpable look of relief that he saw his two traveling companions seated amicably across the table and conversing in low tones. He stood in front of the fire for a few minutes in an effort to get dry.

Their host came back with a tray of cold mutton, a bottle of wine, and three glasses. Bastard rejoined his companions at the table, and the three men commenced their meal. The wine had a raw, slightly bitter taste, and Berini voiced the sentiment of all three.

"Too bad we didn't save some of Henri's magnificent vintage," he said. "We could really use it now."

They reached Nancy at about eleven the following morning and drove through the city in the pouring rain. They stopped for an hour to give the horses a rest and permit Alphonse to buy some provisions. Watching him trudge off in the mud, his cape over his head, Blanc could well imagine his coachman daydreaming about lying in a warm bed with Clarisse instead of sitting up on his box in that downpour and steering their horses along the muddy, treacherous roads.

No one spoke much that morning. Each man seemed wrapped in his own thoughts, as the rain beat its steady tattoo against the roof and sides of the coach, as the vehicle swayed and lurched its way along. It was Berini who finally broke the silence.

"There were one hundred men gathered in the square," he began, without introduction. "They were shivering in the cold, as most of them had been dragged out of their houses with no chance to put on a warm coat. They were of all ages, from youths who didn't yet have beards, to the elderly who needed a cane to walk, to invalids, some of whom had to be carried or helped to the square. The people's representative in charge nodded to the lieutenant, who gave a direct order to his sergeant to commence the execution. The sergeant commanded his troops to raise their muskets and then gave the order to fire.

"The soldiers, about thirty of them, opened fire, and kept shooting, reloading again and again, until not a man was left standing in the square. Then one of the people's representatives called out, 'Let all the wounded stand up; the Republic will pardon them!' Some wounded men did get up, and they were shot down. They were so covered with blood they were unrecognizable. I couldn't tell whether my brother was among them or not. Do you know who the people's representative was who called that out, Inspector Blanc?"

"Desmans," Blanc said.

"Yes, Desmans."

They were silent again. Young Bastard was certainly learning something from this case, Blanc thought to himself. Exactly what it was, he would not venture to guess. What would he himself have done, he wondered, if someone close to him had been murdered? His father, or brother. . . . His father was a sturdy old peasant, still living right outside Salers and still doing a full day's work. He had wanted his son to get an education. His mother died when he was small. Before him, she'd borne her husband two children: a girl, who died in infancy, and a boy, his elder brother, who was killed at the battle of Neerwinden.

What would he have done? Blanc wondered. What would he do now if it happened? The person closest to him in all the world was Daphne. He would like to think that, as a Guardian of the Peace, he'd let the law take its course and not become, as he'd called Berini, "judge, jury, and executioner all rolled into one." But suppose there were no recourse to law, what then? The truth of the matter is that, unless one finds himself in that position, one doesn't know how he'll act. Anything other than that is just empty posturing.

They reached Commercy by evening and stayed at an inn much like the one the night before, where they made do with a scant meal and a cold, uncomfortable room.

Tuesday, November 10, the third day of their journey. The rain continued to come down, but the road was slightly better.

They were coming into the Champagne region now, harvested farmland that was bracing itself for the coming winter.

"M. Berini," Blanc said, "why did you confess?"

"I'm probably going to disillusion you, Chief Inspector," the other replied, "but it wasn't because of your persuasiveness. I believe you were really sincere in your talk about French justice. I just happen to disagree with you."

"Why, then?"

"My good, idealistic friend," Berini said, "do you really think those bad old times are over? Governments change, but people don't. Somewhere in France right now there is another Desmans, another Pardon, another Armand, and another Selvay. They are murderers secondly; first and foremost they are opportunists.

"It wasn't because of your words, but in spite of them, that I confessed. The evidence against me is unimportant. No French government—be it the Republic, the Directory, the Consulate, or the Empire—can afford to let me get away. The prominent men I killed made no secret of their past. They didn't shout it from the rooftops, perhaps, but they didn't try to hide it or lie about it. One of them was a distinguished diplomat, another an outstanding lawyer, a third a successful army contractor, and the fourth a leading maker of church bells. The government certainly knew who they were, what they were, and what they had been. Had there ever been any attempt to bring them to justice? To try them for the slaughter of thousands of innocent people?

"If I were to be found innocent, your government would be found guilty. That is why I want to have my day in court. I want to tell people what I did and why I did it. Perhaps some of them will listen."

The farmlands were left behind. They were passing over a bleak, eroded plain where there were hundreds of grazing sheep. More than once, they found their way blocked by sheep on the road, and Alphonse had to climb down and move them across the road. Nevertheless, they reached Vitry-le-François, on the Marne River, by nightfall.

They were only about 180 kilometers from Paris. The rains

continued to come down, making their progress as slow and difficult as possible. This time it was Blanc who broke the silence in the coach.

"I've been thinking about what you said yesterday, M. Berini. Although I disagree with what you did, I can hardly disagree with what you say. This is to be kept confidential, Bastard; we're talking treason.

"In the middle of the fourteenth century the peasants of France protested because they were hungry. Their ridiculous belief was that they should be able to eat some of the grain they'd sown and harvested, so they refused to till the fields to which they were bound. The response of the nobles was to go out with their hired armies and slaughter them by the thousands. Of course, some of the nobles were killed too. It took more than four centuries for the mass of people to wreak their vengeance upon a class they hated. Is it any wonder that, when that revenge came, it was massive and bloody and largely unjust?

"If the Royalists had their way, we would have another round of repression, followed by another round of bloodletting. Through it all, there would always be the opportunists, as you called them, allying themselves with the winning side, giving and following orders to kill people in the thousands, equally heedless of their victims' guilt or innocence, and doing it legally, according to the laws of the day enacted for that purpose.

"While war often rages around us, we in France have reached an uneasy truce among ourselves. That truce is called the French Empire. I have no idea how long it will last. (This is the treasonable part, you see.) But if it doesn't last, it cannot always be either-or: Empire or chaos. There is, and must be, another way."

"Have you found it?" Berini asked.

"No," Blanc admitted, "and what I have to offer may seem a rather weak solution to a centuries-old problem."

"We still have a long way to go," Berini said, "and plenty of time. Tell me your solution."

Blanc looked out at the rain-sodden landscape for a moment and then resumed his discourse. "Men of reason—men of honor, if you will—have to come together. And there have to be enough of them, of all classes, to ensure that the laws of reason and honor prevail, to see that the opportunists among us don't get another opportunity."

"A noble idea," Berini said. "I quite agree with you. Tell me, Inspector Blanc, how many men of honor do you come into contact with in the daily course of your work?"

"Very few," Blanc admitted. "Yet one finds them in the strangest places, and sometimes where least expected."

"This man whose place I am to take at the guillotine—Léon the Frog. Would you describe him as a man of honor?"

"In his own peculiar way, yes," Blanc replied. "Léon has never carried a weapon; he has never killed or hurt anyone. That is his code of honor, although he wouldn't call it that. He has a girl named Marie Dubois—no relation to our beloved Prefect of Police, Bastard—who, in *her* peculiar way, is devoted to him. Yet when he was running in fear of his life, terrified of being tried and executed for a crime he didn't commit, he wouldn't hide out in Marie's room or go near her. He didn't want to involve her, you see."

"I do see," Berini said. "And if it hadn't been for a certain police inspector, who had *his* peculiar code of honor, Léon the Frog, a thief with a criminal record, would be a corpse in an unmarked grave by now. Well, well." He smiled. "Perhaps there's hope for mankind yet."

They spent the night at a small but clean inn at Sézanne.

Thursday, November 12. It was still raining when they left Sézanne, but more lightly now, and the sky seemed to be clearing. By midafternoon the sky was a perfect blue and the earth was bathed in the sort of sunshine that makes one forget the dank, dismal days that have gone just before. Beneath them, though, the road was still muddy.

"M. Berini," Blanc said, "I have one more question that I haven't asked you yet. What is your real name?"

"I was wondering when you'd ask me that. My real name is Berini. It is the name I created and that I've lived with for so many years I've almost forgotten the one I was born with. That other is an old, honored family name that has never been associated with any crime. I ask that it be kept out of this affair, and further, that if you ever find it out you divulge it to no one. That is my only request."

"I will honor it," Blanc promised him.

By late afternoon of that day, amid a glowing sunset, they reached the eastern barrier of the city of Paris.

There isn't much more to relate in the case of the seven dreamers. Blanc kept his word to the journalist Paul Marais, who received a precise and accurate account of the arrest and the plans and events leading up to it. The *Journal de Paris* therefore had an exclusive story, and Marais's reputation, both with the public and with his fellow scribes, was higher than ever.

Léon Frennel, better known as Léon the Frog, was released from the Prison de l'Hôpital de la Pitié, looking a bit wan but otherwise none the worse for wear. Waiting for him outside was a woman of indeterminate age with a swarthy complexion, whose dark hair had been washed and carefully brushed and who was wearing her Sunday finery for the occasion. As soon as she saw Léon, she rushed at him and alternately hugged him and shook him by the lapels of his coat.

"Léon, I mean it this time," she said, shaking him. "If we don't buy that wineshop now, if you ever, ever steal again, I'll . . . I'll—"

She broke off and leaned sobbing against his shoulder. Léon murmured a few words of comfort, and when he finally calmed her down, the two of them walked off, arms around each other's waists, toward the center of the great city that had given birth to them both and raised them.

The man who was known to the world at large as The Great Berini repeated his confession in a court packed with spectators. Hundreds more had had to be turned away. The three judges sentenced him to be executed. The date of execution was set for Monday, December 14—the earliest legal date. He was incarcerated meantime, as he had been while awaiting trial, at the prison of Meudon.

Chief Inspector Blanc, of the Criminal Investigation Department, found himself back in his own office, seated behind his large mahogany desk, the tricorne standing furled on his right side and a portrait of the Emperor scowling down at him from the wall on his left. Cartier had done a good job in his absence. Fouché was pleased with the outcome of the case, and so, it was reported, was the Emperor. At least, officially they were pleased. What their private thoughts were, they alone knew. Because Berini had admitted his guilt and made a full confession, he was able to make a statement in court, with no one to challenge or interrupt him. Censoring its report in the press was pointless, as over a hundred people had heard him make it, and it would be repeated all over town anyway.

By all rights, Blanc ought to be pleased, and yet he wasn't. There was one great unanswered question, and he wondered whether he would ever find the answer. Know thyself, Socrates had taught, and he thought he did know himself. But there was one question he kept asking, to which he had no answer. If Berini had not killed the women, would he have tried so hard to get him back to France?

On Monday morning, December 14, at 5 o'clock, Berini was executed by guillotine in the courtyard of the prison at Meudon. It was a cold, windy day, and a freezing rain was starting to fall. Because of the publicity the case had received, a sizable crowd was there, despite the early hour and bad weather. All the leading journalists in Paris were present. Blanc didn't attend executions, but he had visited Berini in his cell the week before, at the latter's request.

On Tuesday morning, December 15, Blanc found a sealed letter among the mail on his desk that immediately caught his attention. He recognized the handwriting, as he had seen Berini's written confession. The man must have written it during his last night in his cell, and somehow Blanc felt moved by that knowledge. He broke the seal and opened the letter.

Meudon
14 December, 18—

Chief Inspector Blanc—
    You have won, and once more I congratulate you. But, as you see, I still have the last word!

In these last few weeks, as I have sat here in this cell under the shadow of the guillotine, I have had a great deal of time to think about this whole matter of revenge and bloodlust. I mean the bloodlust of individual men, of mobs, and of whole nations. I'm sure that a cynic would say, if he read this letter, that it is only because I am to be guillotined that I feel this way. But I know that you are not a cynic.

You were right in one of the things you said about me. You said that all of my adult life was centered around the idea of revenge. And that—not what is to happen to me a few hours from now—is what I regret. For a life lived for the sake of revenge is a life wasted.

You spoke also about the cycle of repression and bloody retribution, and your hope that enough men of reason and honor could get together to break that cycle. I hope you find enough such men, my friend. They are sorely needed right now! They will be needed in all places and in all times.

Again, the cynic might point at me and say that I am a fine one to talk, but what has been of most concern to me these past few weeks is when such killings as those that took place at 16 Rue Saint-Guillaume will cease. And here is where your men of reason and honor must shoulder their responsibilities. They must become the leaders of nations, and not remain followers or silent bystanders.

I asked when such killings as those at 16 Rue Saint-Guillaume will cease. They will cease when governments stop killing. They will cease when that monstrosity out there in the courtyard has been disassembled, once and for all. They will cease when atrocities such as those committed at Lyons and Toulon have become faded bloodstains on the pages of history. When there are no fresh bloodstains to take their place. When men, and nations, and governments have come to realize that no cause, however righteous, justifies the spilling of blood. That no ideology, however lofty, is worth the taking of one single human life.

And that, Inspector Blanc, is the last word.

Respectfully yours,
Berini

Bernard St. James was born in Berlin of Romanian parents, was brought up in Paris, and has been, at various times in his life, a disc jockey, a farm laborer, a factory worker, a schoolteacher, and a scriptwriter for U. S. Army Signal Corps training films. He is the author of two previous novels: APRIL THIRTIETH, a historical mystery featuring Inspector Blanc; and THE WITCH, a supernatural novel. He now lives in New York City with his wife, the writer Tiffany Holmes.